**Praise for USA TODAY bestselling author
Kasey Michaels**

"Lots of witty dialogue and humorous situations."
—*RT Book Reviews* on *Suddenly a Bride*

"Funny, down-to-earth and likable characters,
along with snappy dialogue, make this story
one that's hard to put down."
—*RT Book Reviews* on *A Bride After All*

"Kasey Michaels aims for the heart and never misses."
—*New York Times* bestselling author Nora Roberts

"Michaels' new Regency miniseries is a joy.
This wonderful storyteller combines passion, humor,
emotional intensity and depth of characterization with a
devastating secret and attempted murder. She makes it all
work and shows how the power of love can overcome. You
will laugh and even shed a tear over this touching romance."
—*RT Book Reviews* on *How to Tempt a Duke*
(4 ½ stars Top Pick)

"Michaels delivers a poignant and highly satisfying read.
The second Daughtry family book is filled with simmering
sensuality, subtle touches of repartee, a hero out for revenge
and a heroine ripe for adventure. You'll enjoy the ride."
—*RT Book Reviews* on *How to Tame a Lady*

"Michaels has done it again....
Witty dialogue peppers a plot full of delectable details
exposing the foibles and follies of the age."
—*Publishers Weekly,* starred review, on *The Butler Did It*

"[A] hilarious spoof of society wedding rituals wrapped
around a sensual romance filled with crackling dialogue
reminiscent of *The Philadelphia Story.*"
—*Publishers Weekly* on *Everything's Coming Up Rosie*

Dear Reader,

It has been such a pleasure writing about Second Chance Bridal, and I hope you've enjoyed reading the first two books in the trilogy, *A Bride After All* and *Suddenly a Bride*.

If so, you've already met Chessie Burton, owner of Second Chance Bridal, and her friend Marylou Smith-Bitters (one of my favorite characters ever!).

Well, now it's time for left-at-the-altar Chessie to find her true love, her own second chance. And if Marylou has anything to do with it, we're in for a fun ride!

Come along as Chessie discovers a passionate side of herself she didn't think she had, and a handsome contractor looking for anything but love gets the surprise of his life!

Enjoy!

Kasey Michaels

THE BRIDE PLAN

KASEY MICHAELS

Harlequin®

SPECIAL EDITION

Recycling programs
for this product may
not exist in your area.

ISBN-13: 978-0-373-65591-5

THE BRIDE PLAN

Copyright © 2011 by Kathryn Seidick

This edition published by arrangement with Harlequin Books S.A.

For questions and comments about the quality of this book please contact us at Customer_eCare@Harlequin.ca.

www.eHarlequin.com

Printed in U.S.A.

To my pal Joan Hohl—because it has been a while…

Prologue

Elizabeth Hollingswood sat on a blanket on the grassy hillside overlooking the baseball diamond, her friends Claire and Nick Barrington occupying the next blanket. The sun was bright, the freshly mowed grass smelled wonderful and the small white petals of the flowering crab trees that lined the street bordering the ball field, loosened by the breeze, made Elizabeth think of a soft, fragrant snow shower. It was a perfect afternoon. Well, at least for those not suffering from pollen allergies, she corrected mentally as Nick sneezed.

It was another spring, and another Grasshopper baseball season. Elizabeth smiled as she watched her husband, Will, going through the signals from the third-base coaching box, first touching a finger to his nose, then to his chin, and then tipping his cap before rubbing a hand across his chest and beginning again, the signals now to cap, chin, nose.

"Look at Mikey just standing there at the plate with that dazed expression on his face," Elizabeth said, sighing as she reached for her bottle of water. "He doesn't have a clue what Will is trying to tell him to do."

Nick grinned at her. "I think I've got it about figured out. He's either telling him to bunt...or blow his nose. Ah, here we go. The direct approach."

Elizabeth watched as Will called for time, and then motioned for Mikey to meet him halfway along the baseline. A whispered conversation accompanied by more cryptic hand gestures followed; Mikey returned to the plate and promptly struck out, ending the game.

"Well," Nick said, standing up, and then helping his pregnant wife to her feet, "that wasn't so bad. Fourteen to two."

"You can say that," Elizabeth groused. "You don't have to go home with the coach and the kid who made the last out. If Danny says one wrong word to his brother I'm going to have to murder him. For the second time this week," she added as she folded the blanket.

The twins, Mikey and Danny, along with Sean, Nick's son from his first marriage, ambled up the hill to gather the fruit and juice boxes it had been Claire's duty to provide as team mom for the day.

"You okay, Mikey?" Elizabeth asked him quietly.

"Sure, Mom. Pops says it was his fault for telling me

to swing. Gotta go, we have to collect the bases and hand out the treats."

Claire looked over at Elizabeth. "Pops? That's new, isn't it?"

Elizabeth nodded, feeling her cheeks flush. Her first husband, Jamie, father of the twins, had died nearly six years ago, and her marriage to Will was not quite a year old. "They said they felt *funny* calling him Will, and all the other kids have dads. But they didn't want to forget their own dad, so they came up with Pops. Will doesn't say much about it, but I know he's pleased. So am I. Kids need to be kids."

"I think it's terrific. Sean's mother is still in the picture, although not as much as any of us would like, so I'm Claire to Sean. But sometimes he slips. I don't say anything about it, either. But, yes, I'm pleased. Uh-oh, here comes Marylou. Look at her trying not to do a flip in those high heels. Do you think there's something wrong at the shop? I hope nothing's happened to Chessie."

Marylou Smith-Bitters, thrice-married socialite and now not only Chessie Burton's good friend but also part owner of Second Chance Bridal and Wedding Planners, did a quick two-step down the grassy slope before grabbing on to Elizabeth's arm to stop herself from a headlong plunge down the remainder of the hill.

"I'm so glad I found you both together," she said rather breathlessly. "We've got a problem. A *b-i-i-g* problem."

Elizabeth, who had taken a part-time job at Second Chance a few months earlier, replacing Eve D'Allesandro, who had taken off for the south of France with Elizabeth's employer, the novelist Richard Halstead, sighed and shook her head. "It's Doreen Nesbit again, isn't it? You'd think that by the time you got to your third groom, you'd learn to pick one who isn't a control freak. He's had her change the table favors three times already."

Marylou waved her fire-engine-red-tipped fingers as if erasing Doreen Nesbit from the conversation. "This isn't about the business—and, no, he didn't change the favors again. I told him I'd tell Doreen about his little friend who works at the ice creamery on Broad Street if he tried." She took a deep breath and let it out dramatically. "Here's the deal, and it's deadly serious. Chessie has to get married."

Elizabeth and Claire exchanged puzzled glances, which left it up to Nick to put his foot in his mouth all by himself: "She's pregnant? I didn't even know she was dating anyone."

The puzzled glances turned to twin expressions of female disgust.

"One, husband mine, pregnancy does not mean an automatic walk down the aisle. And two...well, you're right. Chessie hasn't had a date since the last time Will set her up and she made us all promise to kill her first if we ever got it into our heads to set her up again."

"Are we done?" Marylou asked, adjusting the pearls at her throat. "Ready to get back to the problem? Which means, by the way, listening to me."

By this time Will had joined them, and Elizabeth

quickly put a finger to his lips before he could say anything. Clearly Marylou was on a mission, and when Marylou was on a mission people with an even cursory sense of self-preservation stayed out of her way.

"It's Richard Peters," Marylou said, and then sighed for dramatic effect. "He called the shop an hour ago. He called last week, but I thought I'd gotten rid of him by saying Chessie moved to Boston and I was the new owner of the shop. Anyway, Missy took the message and was about to deliver it to Chessie when I intercepted her. The child nearly swallowed her gum, which she knows full well she's not supposed to chew within five miles of the wedding gowns."

Will, who happened to also be Chessie's cousin, slipped his arm around Elizabeth's waist, which was rapidly disappearing as she was now six months pregnant. "Rick Peters, Marylou? It isn't an uncommon name. Doesn't mean it's him."

"What am I missing here? Who's Rick Peters?"

"Nick, shhh," Claire warned quietly. "We're in the role of audience here."

"Rick Peters is the guy who left Chessie at the altar so he could run off and elope with the maid of honor," Elizabeth whispered.

"Damn."

"Oh, please, Claire," Marylou said, "you're being too polite. I can think of much better words. And it *is* that Rick Peters, Will, because his message was that he wanted Chessie to know he's moved back to Allentown and he'd like to take her to dinner. The man is scum. And you know what's going to happen, don't you?"

"Chessie might say yes," Will said, nodding his head as if in agreement with what Marylou *hadn't* said. "That's always been her problem. She's too damn nice. It's been six years or so, and I'd still like to bust the guy one in the chops."

"We could form a line, and all of us take a shot at him," Marylou agreed, "but that isn't going to solve anything."

"And getting Chessie married would?" Elizabeth asked, feeling she'd at last gotten a firm grip on Marylou's strategy. "Isn't that just a little bit drastic?"

"Drastic times call for drastic measures," Marylou pronounced. "Now, it only took me twenty minutes to drive over here, so maybe my plan doesn't have all the bugs worked out of it yet, but here's what I'm thinking."

"This should be good," Nick said, earning him a jab in the ribs from his loving wife.

"We're all going to find Chessie a prospective groom. *All* of us," she stressed, glaring at Nick. "Even you, Will, although you really need to cultivate a more acceptable circle of male friends to draw from, Counselor. Chessie says if she sees another lawyer she's going to have to hurt you.

"Anyway, that's the plan. We keep Chessie so busy with blind dates and discreet setups that she has no time to listen to Rick Peters tell her what a huge mistake he made and how now he wants her back. Because we all know how that works—they always want back what they once had and then tossed away. Men are so predictable it's almost embarrassing."

"He's divorced?" Claire asked, but then shook her head. "Never mind, of course he is. I won't even ask how you know that, Marylou. Sorry for the interruption. Go on, please."

Marylou smiled, rubbing her palms together as she neatly stepped into the role of general of this campaign she'd concocted. "Peters isn't just visiting. He's back to stay. Which means we have to get Chessie settled, sooner rather than later. Agreed? We'll call it TBP—The Bride Plan. Each one of us produces a prospective groom. We'll make up a schedule so we don't accidentally double book Chessie for the same date. If we find enough of them, one of them is bound to stick, right?"

"Like bubble gum to a wedding gown," Elizabeth said quietly.

"She'll thank us one day," Marylou said, her smile now only slightly apprehensive. She looked at her friends for reassurance. "Won't she?"

Chapter One

Chessie Burton turned the sign in the window from Open to Closed and wearily began making her way toward the stairs to her apartment, situated above Second Chance Bridal and Wedding Planners.

Eight months had all but flown past since Chessie and her friend Marylou had decided they'd expand Chessie's business by also offering wedding-planning services to their clients.

The logic had been unassailable.

First-time brides often took a year or more to plan their weddings; they had family and lots of pals to help them make their big day perfect.

Second-chance brides? Not so much. Second-chance brides often had kids, car pools, soccer practice or ballet class, a full-time job and a much shorter time frame between "Okay, let's do it" and "I do." This was why Chessie always maintained such an extensive in-stock bridal-gown selection; ordering in a gown that might take six to twelve weeks to arrive often didn't work well for second-chance brides.

So, in theory, branching out to wedding planning had seemed a great idea. Marylou could be very persuasive, and thanks to her husband Ted's considerable wealth and eagerness to please his wife in all things, financing the project had been no problem.

In practice, however, the idea had turned into a case of too much of a good thing. Chessie and Marylou had found themselves pretty much on call 24/7, which didn't make Marylou's husband all that happy, and Chessie was spending entirely too many nights sitting cross-legged on the floor in front of her TV, dealing with trays of sugared almonds and net doilies and tiny little bows and a hot-glue gun.

It was great that Elizabeth had stepped in to replace Eve, and Missy, their teenage part-timer, had shown a remarkable talent for concocting spreadsheets that kept each wedding's to-do list organized and up-to-date. Berthe, longtime Second Chance Bridal seamstress, had volunteered to help out on the sales floor as well, and Marylou often seemed to be everywhere at once, putting out small fires before they could become conflagrations.

But none of that got the boxes and boxes of supplies out of Chessie's apartment, her beloved private sanctuary, and she had adamantly refused to relocate somewhere other than the huge Victorian home she had bought and furnished and simply adored.

Chessie waded through the crowded living room, eyeing the boxes holding three new albums of wedding-invitation samples that had arrived a week ago, promising herself she'd unbox them tonight after she'd eaten dinner…if she could find the kitchen. Thank God they were going to start that addition soon, to make a dedicated workspace and also to house all of this stuff.

She paused in the hallway and turned to look at her reflection in the full-length mirror that hung there because she'd hadn't found any better place for it.

She looked tired. She was tired. Her coppery hair had pretty much outgrown its careful shaping, and looked more wild than artfully disheveled. She put her hands to her pale cheeks, wondering when last she'd seen the sun, and sighed as she looked at the huge blue eyes that were looking back at her, shiny with tears.

Rick was back in town. Chessie knew this because she'd found a note next to the telephone, scribbled by Missy. Rick was back in town and wanted to meet with her, have dinner. His phone number was scribbled beneath the message. She knew the number. He was back living with his parents. Was that pitiful, some sort of twisted poetic justice, or was it more pitiful that she still had the number committed to memory?

The last time she'd seen him had been six years, three months and twelve days ago—she'd worked that out in her head earlier. They'd just left the rehearsal dinner, her maid of honor and best friend walking with them into the parking lot. He'd apologized for not driving Chessie home, but he had something he had to do. He'd intimated that it was a surprise, and she'd been certain it had something to do with their honeymoon in Cape Cod, because he'd hinted as much.

She'd laughed, told him she loved him, wrapped her arms around his neck and kissed him soundly—a kiss he'd returned with considerable fervor and a bit of pleasant groping that suggested the last thing he wanted was to leave her alone for the rest of the evening. Then she watched him walk toward his car.

And out of her life.

"How do you do that, Rick?" she asked the empty apartment as she entered the kitchen, flipping on the overhead light. "How do you all but make love to one woman, while another woman is standing there watching, the same woman you'll be taking to Mexico with you on a midnight flight? How does someone's best friend watch something like that, and then drive her supposed best friend home and say she'll be back in the morning to help her get dressed for the wedding? What kind of monsters were you, both of you? And what kind of blind victim was I, not to have seen it all coming?"

It had been years since Chessie had thought about either Rick or Diana. She wished she wasn't thinking about either of them right now, but sometimes a mind wouldn't turn off just because you wanted it to. So, as she spread peanut butter on two slices of fresh bread and then slapped the two pieces together, she attempted to concentrate on the positives.

She wouldn't have Second Chance Bridal if it weren't for Rick and Diana. She's started the business with her own unused wedding gown as the first piece of stock, and it had turned out to be the very first gown she'd sold. She loved her business, loved the friends she'd made, the life she'd built.

She wouldn't have any of that if she'd married Rick.

Chessie took a bite out of her sandwich and then quickly poured herself a glass of iced tea, hoping to get that bite unstuck from the roof of her mouth. Jelly helped to cut peanut butter so that it wasn't so sticky, wasn't a choking hazard. She knew that, but she'd forgotten. Granted, she didn't want to see Rick again, but suicide by peanut butter wasn't on her agenda, either.

Still munching on her dinner, Chessie threaded her way to the bedroom, stripped off her clothing and stepped under the shower, swallowing her last bite of the sandwich.

Once in the T-shirt and running shorts that served as both casual wear and pajamas, her hair still damp and forming itself into the natural burnished curls she'd have to straighten in the morning, she retraced her steps to the living room, glared at the three large boxes that seemed to be staring right back at her and searched the floor for the TV remote. Maybe she'd just lie down and watch a sitcom or something before she got to work, because it was going to be another long night.

Not that she was lonely. She was simply alone. Being alone hadn't been her choice six years ago, but it was now.

Jace Edwards considered himself a self-made man. He'd begun working construction as a teenager, and over the ensuing years he'd learned how to do any job the members of his crew could do, often better. It hadn't happened quickly or easily, had probably helped destroy his marriage, but the Edwards Construction Company was still his baby, and he was a very proud father.

It was just past 7:00 a.m. and he'd already had his third cup of coffee. He made it a rule to always be on-site for the first day of any new job, and today's job hadn't been an exception, even if the idea of running into Marylou Smith-Bitters's business partner wasn't something he was looking forward to, not by the way Marylou had described Ms. Chessie Burton.

It wasn't any one thing Marylou had said, but more of an impression he'd got listening to her. Chessie Burton was driven, successful, particular, didn't want her customers disturbed with a lot of noise and was extremely concerned with the amount of dust and mess that might accompany the construction.

As if construction could be kept noise- and dust-free. Get real, lady!

If he hadn't needed the work, he might have turned

down the job. Second Chance Bridal? Why didn't they call it what it really was? Strike Two Bridal. The whole concept was pretty creepy when you got right down to it. Or maybe his own Strike One had made him leery of any place that catered to people like himself—marital losers.

In any case, in his mind, Jace had conjured up a middle-aged woman with her hair in a bun and a pair of reading glasses hanging from a strap around her neck. She'd be on his case for the month it would take to put the two-story addition on the house that, if Jace were the owner, would have remained exactly the way it was, which was perfect. He loved these old Queen Anne Victorians, even owned one himself.

"You want to tell me again how we're going to build everything first, and only then break through the walls?"

Jace turned to look at his head framer, who was holding the unrolled plans in his hands and looking confused.

"I know it's the hard way, Carl. The back of the house consists of the owner's bedroom and bath upstairs and, downstairs, the room where they store the wedding gowns and all that stuff. We can't just rip out those walls and have them open to the elements until we get the job done. Not to mention the noise."

"Uh-huh," Carl said, nodding. "But we are going to strip off the siding before the new walls go up, get rid of the shutters, the rain gutters, right? Tie in to the electricity and plumbing, since there's going to be another bathroom? Then just cut in the two doors giving access to the building, right, cutting through those two existing windows? No way we can do any of that without some noise and dirt. We're not knitting a sweater here, Jace. The owner knows that, right?"

Before Jace could answer there came the shrill beeping sound of a warning signal and the rumble from the engine of a piece of heavy equipment backing up into the yard along the cement driveway. This was followed hard by the squeal of massive air brakes, the grinding noise of gears meshing, lifting and then loudly depositing the large metal Dumpster that would hold the construction waste. The ground beneath them actually shook a little from the impact.

"I'd say she does now," Jace said, grinning. "Okay, get the guys up on the ladders and start stripping off that siding. I'll be back later to see how it's going."

He'd almost made it to the alley at the back of the yard, and to his car, when he saw her. Her appearance hit his brain in separate bursts of information. Coppery curls tumbling wildly around a pale oval face. Eyes as blue as the summer sky and big as quarters at the moment. A slim, trim, not-too-tall body, with pinup-calendar-worthy legs that went up to her ears. A chest that heaved up and down interestingly as she seemed to be trying to catch her breath. She wasn't wearing a bra under that T-shirt, either. *Nice*. Bare feet. A TV remote clutched in her right hand.

A TV remote?

"Wh-*what* do you think you're doing?"

Nice voice, he added mentally. Sort of husky. Sexy. Possibly slightly tinged with homicidal rage, but still sexy.

"Uh—Jace?" Carl said, backing up as the woman advanced on him. "You wanna come back here a minute?"

Jace tipped back his baseball cap as he approached, holding on to the bill as he said, "Ma'am. Your neighbor didn't tell you we were beginning construction today?"

"Neighbor? What neighbor? I—" she gestured rather wildly toward the building "—I own this place."

This was Chessie Burton? For the next four weeks or so, he could come to the job site and she'd be here? Every day? *And who said the gods weren't kind?*

"So you're Chessie Burton? Marylou's business partner?"

"No. Marylou is my business partner. I'm the senior part— Oh, who cares? I *live* here. You should have checked with me before you started playing the "Anvil Chorus" on the back of my house."

He could kiss her. Right here, right now, for no good reason he could think of, Jace really wanted to kiss her. She was so damned cute…

"What's the matter? Why are you grinning like that? And another thing—who the hell are you? Do you know it's only seven freaking o'clock in the morning? What do you do for an encore—march a brass band through here? Maybe some elephants bringing up the rear?"

"Name's Jace. Jace Edwards. Elephants? Let me guess. Not a morning person, are you?" Jace asked, doing his best not to laugh. God, she was magnificent. A little on the wacko side of normal, maybe, but he hadn't seen anything this good in the morning—or at any time, come to think of it—in a long, long time. Maybe never.

She rolled those big blue eyes. "Oh, he made a funny. Ha. Ha."

The sound of industrious hammering and ripping of siding quickly followed. Clearly, Carl and the crew had heard enough.

She waved the TV remote in Jace's face, then seemed to realize she was holding what might be construed as a weapon, and lowered her arm. "Make…them…stop."

"You don't want the addition?" He was being mean to a clearly upset woman, but he couldn't help himself.

"No—yes! Yes, I want the addition. I just don't want it at seven o'clock in the morning. I don't want anything at seven o'clock in the morning, at least not until I've had my coffee, damn it! And stop grinning at me like that. What did you say your name was again?"

"Jace," he told her, this time leaving off the Edwards as he held out his hand to her. "And you're Chessie Burton. I think Marylou and I had some miscommunication when we met here two weeks ago to plan out the job. In a couple of ways."

"Uh-huh," Chessie said, holding out her own hand, and then quickly transferring the remote to her left palm before she shook hands with him. "I was working a wedding and couldn't be here. Look, I don't want to get off on the wrong foot here, and I'm sure you and Marylou will work together just fine, but one minute I was asleep, and the next I thought the world was about to end. I'm not usually so...so fierce."

"Apology accepted, Ms. Burton."

"That wasn't an apology, it was an explanation," she said, turning mulish again.

"Okay. And while you're explaining—what's with the TV remote?"

"I fell asleep on the couch last night," she said quietly, her freckled cheeks blushing a pretty pink. "I don't know why I'm holding the stupid thing. Are you going to start every morning at seven?"

"I'll talk with the guys. Maybe they'll want to go eight to six instead of seven to five. Of course, then Carl over there won't be able to pick up his grandson from his day care, and Jimmy's a newlywed, and you know how new brides are. Oh, and George has to get home because his wife works part-time at—"

"All right, all right, I get it. You start at seven. At least now I'll be prepared."

"But hopefully not armed," Jace said, actually feeling a little sorry for her. Nobody liked to wake up thinking the world was about to end. But not sorry enough to keep him from beginning to unbutton his shirt, because he wasn't blind, and he'd noticed how she'd been looking at him. Faintly mad...but at least marginally interested.

Which was good, because he was feeling pretty *interested* himself. It was a good enough reason for making a jerk of himself, if he were still in high school. But what the hell. "Now, if you'll excuse me, Ms. Burton, I've got to get to work."

Chessie's eyes widened slightly as she watched him strip out of his shirt and toss it over an azalea bush that was still blooming. Smiling, he grabbed a short pry-bar from Jimmy's tool belt and headed for the rear of the house even as she was making a pretty fast retreat back down the path to the side door leading into the Victorian.

Safety glasses in place, he inserted the pry-bar and began stripping off a length of siding, the morning sun feeling good against his bare back.

"I thought Bob was going to be on-site. You working this job yourself, Jace?" Carl asked in confusion.

"I am now. Bob can take over for me at the Carter house. If that's all right with you, of course."

"She is cute, I'll give you that," Carl said, getting back to business. "I just didn't think you'd noticed."

"Oh, I noticed," Jace said, giving the siding another rip.

"A four-man crew?" Carl persisted. "We'll get done faster than we thought. The boys and I were hoping for a full month's work on this one."

"Do I look like a man in a hurry to you, Carl?"

The older man laughed and slapped Jace on the back. "Why, you dog, you. You really did notice."

* * *

Chessie held the phone to her ear, listening to the rings. "Pick up. Pick up, pick up. Pick-up-pick-up-pick— Marylou! Why didn't you tell me?"

"Chessie? Is that you?" Marylou asked, her voice gravelly with sleep.

"Yes, it's me. Why didn't you tell me construction started today? At the crack of dawn! And that man, that Jace something-or-other? Why didn't you tell me about him?"

"Jace Edwards? What about him? Wait. Hold on a sec while I get up, go in the other room. No, Ted, nothing's wrong. It's just Chessie. Go back to sleep, darling. Okay, now I'm in the hall and he's already snoring again. That man sleeps with the easy innocence of a baby, I swear it. Only louder. Now, what about Jace Edwards?"

"Oh, come on, Marylou. I wasn't born yesterday. That wavy black hair you'd love to run your fingers through, those light gray eyes that have those sexy smile crinkles around them. That tan. That tall Greek-god body—he stripped to his waist, Marylou. Right in front of me! Shoulders that go from here to there, a waist without a single inch-to-pinch of fat hanging over his belt. Washboard abs, isn't that what they're called?"

"I guess so. He didn't strip for me, darn it, but your mental picture is almost as good. The man is a hunk. So where's the problem?"

"The problem, Marylou-the-matchmaker, depends on whether or not you checked out his *real* credentials. The ones that matter. You know, the ones where we find out if he's any good at his job. This is my house he's tearing into. I want to know if he knows how to hammer a nail into a stud, not that he *is* a stud. Oh, God, that's sounds bad, even for me. But you know what I mean."

"Jace comes very highly recommended, Chessie. And I am *not* matchmaking. I gave up on that long ago. I had some success with Claire and Nick, but you're a hard case. I've taken the pledge, no more trying to set up Chessie, okay? I want to keep my success ratio high."

Chessie finally subsided onto one of the stools at the breakfast bar that made up one side of her kitchen. "I overreacted," she said, lowering her head into her hand. "Made an idiot of myself. I'm sorry."

She wasn't sure, wouldn't be able to swear to it in any court, but she got the feeling she could actually *hear* Marylou's smile, and she hung up as soon as she could.

What was the matter with her? Oh, okay, so her house was being ripped apart, and her routine along with it. But that was to be expected. She'd just been surprised, the noise had startled her out of a deep sleep. She could be forgiven for that, or at least she could rationalize her actions to herself.

But who could rationalize her reaction to Jace Edwards.

"That was bad," she told herself as she headed for the shower. "That was very, very bad. Another minute and you would have looked like a construction-worker groupie, if there is such a thing. From now on, Chessie Burton, you are going to avoid the man."

If you have to tie yourself to the mast and have your eyes covered and your ears blocked up, just like that mythological Greek guy did when he faced the Sirens, she added mentally, right before opting for a cold shower.

Chapter Two

"**I** said," Chessie repeated, this time half screaming the words, "you look beautiful in that gown! The mermaid style is *perfect* for you!"

Oh, brother. How was she supposed to sell gowns, make her brides feel special, when she had to shout over the sounds of hammering and electric saws and—she nearly jumped out of her skin as somebody dropped what sounded like a half ton of boards all at one time.

Helen Metcalf looked into the three-sided mirror and shook her head. "The style is good, but there's not enough bling. At my age, I need some bling, to take the attention away from my crepey neck."

"You don't have a creepy neck," Chessie assured her, once more speaking over the noise of an electric saw.

"I hope not! I said *crepe,* not creep. Anyway, I don't think this is the one. Then again, it's so difficult to concentrate with all that noise. What's going on out there?"

As she helped Helen out of the gown, Chessie explained about the construction that had already been going on for an endless three days, and would continue for at least another month, or so Marylou kept telling her.

"Ooh, construction workers. With tool belts and tight jeans and bare chests. Lead me to them," Helen said, heading for the window in her strapless bra, French-cut silk panties and little else. She pulled back the drapery and leaned her head to one side, looking toward the rear of the building. "Oh. My. *God.*"

Chessie twisted her hands together in front of her, longing to punch something. Or someone. He was out there without his shirt again, the great big show-off. Jace Edwards. Owner of Edwards Construction, owner of his own built-in six-pack, and all round pain in her rump. Helen wasn't the only person to have had that oh-my-god reaction, one way or another, to Jace Edwards.

"He's just a man without a shirt, Helen."

"No, my Joe is just a man without a shirt. *That* out there is a whole 'nother story, that's what that is. Can you just imagine him with butter on top?"

Chessie had to laugh. "Helen, you're getting married."

Slowly, reluctantly, Helen backed away from the

window. "Right, married, which isn't the same as dead, even if it felt like it with my ex. I'm still allowed to look, I just can't touch. Have you? You know—touched?"

No, but not for lack of thinking about it, Chessie said inside her head. Outside her head, she said, "Not interested."

"Really? Are you ill?"

Chessie blinked. "No—why?"

"Because if you're not at least a little bit interested in *that,* maybe you want to consider vitamins or something."

"I can't believe you teach kindergarten," Chessie said, motioning for Helen to raise her arms so another mermaid-style gown could be dropped over her head. "What a potty mouth you have."

"It's a part of my girlish charm. Ah," she said, smoothing her hands down over her hips as Chessie did up the concealed zipper. "Now, this is more like it. I love the neckline, and the way it seems to give me a shape, which I'd pretty much thought I'd lost after the third kid." She turned about to see the sweep of the demi-train, and then turned back to stand foursquare in front of the mirror.

And didn't say another word for a full minute.

Chessie recognized the signs. She quickly grabbed the elbow-length veil and secured it to Helen's blond curls and then handed her a bouquet of deep-purple-silk calla lilies.

Then she handed her a tissue.

"This is the one, isn't it?" she said after Helen wiped her cheeks and blew her nose.

Helen nodded, clearly not trusting her voice. For all the woman's bravado, her insistence that it was only a second wedding, a formality really, and she didn't expect to feel "special," Helen Metcalf was suddenly feeling special. Every bride deserved to feel that way.

Chessie handed her over to Berthe to discuss built-in bras and how to bustle the small train for the reception, and headed for her office, deliberately averting her eyes from the door leading to the side yard and, if she simply made a left, to the back of the house and the construction.

She inspected the progress each night, after Jace and his crew departed, but she had made it a point not to go outside while they were on-site. Not to offer them a pitcher of iced tea, not to ask any questions, not to complain about the noise…and definitely not to peek at Jace Edwards sans shirt.

Okay, once. Yesterday afternoon. Just that once she'd sneaked upstairs and looked out the third-floor attic window, just in time to see him holding up the garden hose over his head, rinsing himself off to stay cool she supposed, and then shaking his head like a dog to rid himself of the excess water. She'd thought, *I could lick it off,* and then mentally slapped herself upside the head, because she didn't think that way. Who thought that way?

Helen Metcalf, probably. That woman had more fun in her mind than Chessie had awake and upright.

One hand on the doorknob to her office, a thought struck Chessie. By staying away, wasn't she making it pretty obvious that there was a reason she was staying away? After all, any normal person wanted to see what's going on when the thing that was having something going on with it was her very own house, her very own business.

Why, he was probably out there right now, laughing at her, thinking he'd scared her away.

The nerve of the man!

She took the stairs two at a time and headed for her kitchen and the full pitcher of iced tea she had just happened to make that morning because... Well, it didn't matter why she'd made it. She dumped the ice out of a tray and into the pitcher. She tucked a stack of tall plastic cups under her arm, grabbed the pitcher and headed back down the steps before she could change her mind.

Over to the door. Out onto the three concrete steps leading down to the concrete path that led to the rear of the house. Down the concrete path, the cups beginning to slip out from under her arm. Around the corner to the picnic table they'd pushed over to the fence and out of the way.

All done without thinking, because thinking was dangerous. Almost more dangerous than counting up the muscles on Jace Edwards's rib cage and getting to, yup, solid six-pack.

"Anyone thirsty?" she called out, smiling at the crew

in general, her gaze sliding over the four men, landing on none of them. "I've got some iced tea."

All four men put down their tools and approached the picnic table, three of them murmuring thanks as they took turns pouring iced tea, and then heading for the shade of the red maple at the back of the yard.

Jace Edwards poured himself a cup as well, but then stayed where he was. Which was much too close to Chessie. He smelled like sun and some spicy cologne and a little good old manly sweat, and she had to clear her throat before she could talk to his chest...she winced, lifted her head to readjust her gaze...before she could talk to him.

"How—how's it going?"

"Not as well as we could have hoped," he told her, and then drained the glass in a few manly gulps as she watched his throat work and felt suddenly quite thirsty herself. "You've got some dry rot we have to take care of before we go much further. Some wet rot, too. Both kinds. I told Marylou yesterday when she was here. She told you?"

"No," Chessie said, looking worriedly at her house. "She didn't tell me. How bad?"

"We won't know that until we check a little more, but I don't think it could be too extensive."

"As in not too extensive to be too expensive?"

He smiled at her. Those light gray eyes—she hadn't known she could like light gray eyes—sort of twinkled as the laugh lines around them crinkled. "That, too. You've had some water, rain most likely, get in between the original siding and the add-on. And the original siding, being wood, started to grow some mold. The rain gutter was pulled away a bit along the lower back roof, probably from all that ice we had last winter. The slate on the roof is good, nearly indestructible, so at least you've got that in your favor."

"There's *mold* under my siding? Isn't that dangerous?" Chessie plunked herself down on the picnic-table bench, figurative dollar signs circling just above her head. "Does all the siding have to come down?"

"That's the good news. The siding is already down. That's how we saw the mold damage and got rid of it, replaced all the damaged boards. What it means, mostly, is you were hearing a lot more ripping and hammering the past two days than you probably counted on."

"I didn't count on any ripping and hammering," she admitted quietly. "I was sort of hoping it would all happen magically. You know, like little elves showing up in the night, and the next thing I'd know I'd have an addition."

"Little elves? With little tool belts? Tiny little velvet-covered hammers?"

"Magic wands, actually," Chessie said, trying not to smile. "And wings. Don't forget the wings."

"I'm trying to picture Carl with wings." He shook his head. "Nope, not happening."

"I don't think the look would be too good on you, either. Although the pointed shoes might be interesting.

Look. I…I, um, I'm sorry about the other morning. We sort of got off on the wrong foot, didn't we?"

He smiled that I-know-what-you're-thinking-and-I might-be-thinking-it-too smile again. Damn, his teeth were white! She tried to picture him standing in front of his bathroom mirror, struggling to apply whitening strips like in the commercials, but that image wouldn't form, either. He was just one of those naturally drop-dead-gorgeous human beings. She shouldn't blame him, he probably couldn't help it.

"I don't know. I thought it was…interesting. I've never before been attacked by a TV remote."

"I usually make a better first impression. Although you probably should be glad I didn't fall asleep holding the glue gun."

"I can think of better things to take to bed with you than a glue gun."

Chessie felt her cheeks going hot. She wasn't going to touch that statement with a ten-foot pole. "I didn't fall asleep watching TV in bed. I fell asleep on the couch because I was supposed to be making little bows and sticking them on— Never mind. Let's just say my life is going to get easier once this addition is done and I have an actual workroom."

"About that. I was only inside the building the day Marylou and I took the tour. Since then, I've been working from the measurements and drawings I made that day, and I think I might have a better suggestion now for the egress from your bedroom to the upstairs workroom.

You'd have more wall space for shelving, which I think you'll probably want to have in there."

"Really? I, um, I guess we could go inside and you could…check that out?" *My bedroom? He wants me to lead him to my bedroom? Hoo-doggies, I couldn't have just stayed inside and let them find their own iced tea?*

"That would be the plan. If you don't mind? Marylou explained that you didn't want anyone inside during business hours until it was totally necessary. We're halfway through the framing, and as soon as we're under roof, it's going to be necessary. Let me get my plans, and I'll meet you inside."

He was reaching for his shirt as she nodded and headed back down the cement path, her mind retracing her steps this morning as she got dressed and raced downstairs for an early delivery. She knew she hadn't made up her bed, but she didn't really care about that. It was what she'd done with the clothes she'd stripped out of last night before she'd gotten into that bed that she couldn't remember.

All she'd need would be for Jace Edwards to ask to see her room for some reason, and then let him walk in there to see her leopard-skin-patterned underwire bra dangling from the doorknob to her bathroom. That was a visual to make her carefully straightened hair curl.

Once inside, she broke into a run, climbing the stairs in record time to do a quick grab-and-stash of anything she didn't want him to see. She'd just grabbed the bra from exactly where she'd left it—hanging on that doorknob—when she heard a knock against the door frame in the living room.

"The lady downstairs said I could come up. Chessie?"

"Yes, I'm here. Come on back."

She lifted her pillow and shoved the bra beneath it, and then quickly sat down on the side of the bed.

Then just as quickly sprang back up again, as if the mattress was on fire. Was she out of her mind? Who sat on a bed when a man was on his way into the room? Women with ideas in their heads that didn't belong there, that's who!

Jace stuck his head and shoulders around the doorway, and then smiled. He was wearing his shirt, she'd give him that much. But he couldn't have buttoned it? "Hi, again. I brought the plans and a measuring tape. Are you sure I'm not disturbing you too much?"

Oh, the many ways she could take that statement!

"No, no, it's fine." She turned in a small circle, her hands sort of aimlessly fluttering until she stopped them by entwining her fingers until her knuckles probably showed white. "*Mi casa es su casa* for the duration, or whatever. You were, uh, talking shelves?"

"Yes, a sort of combination hallway and storage area. Instead of the door opening directly into the workroom. Too boxy, you know? I was taking the easy way out, I guess. Here, let me show you." He unrolled the plans, blueprints, whatever they were, and laid them on the bed. When the large, crinkly papers tried to roll into a cylinder once more, he picked up a sneaker that had found its home on the floor last night, and placed it on the left edge of the papers.

Then he moved to grab the pillow and use it to hold down the other edge He'd half lifted it before she could react.

"No!" Chessie grabbed his hand, then quickly let it go, as if it was also too hot to handle. "That probably won't work. Feather pillow, you know. Too, er, too light. I…I'll just sit here and hold them down."

"Okay," Jace said, looking at her in some confusion. "You're a funny girl."

"That's what I'm told. A real laugh a minute," she said through clenched teeth and a smile that hurt her cheeks. "So, uh—these are the plans?"

Commanding herself to calm down and—for God's sake—shut up, Chessie did her best to listen, nod in the right places and pretend she didn't notice that he was only two feet away from her. Not exactly invading her personal space, but since this particular personal space happened to be her bedroom…well, yeah, maybe he was. Him and his cologne and his open shirt and his laugh lines and his…no, she wouldn't think about his bare chest. She'd never had a thing for bare chests, not ever. On her list of what attracted her to men, bare chests wasn't even in the top five. So why was she so suddenly fixated on his?

"And then I figure we can paint it all purple and put a cherry on top."

"Uh-huh— *What?*"

"Then you are listening. I wasn't sure."

She got to her feet, the crinkling sound of the plans rolling back into their cylinder shape closely following. "Oh, cripes, I'm sorry. I wasn't listening. Could…could you maybe just…back up a little?"

"I could," he said, not moving. "But we probably ought to get this over with."

"The…" She cleared her throat. Honestly, she was never at a loss for words. If anything, she talked too much. Just ask her cousin Will, he'd tell him. "You mean…talking about the plans?"

Jace took a small step closer, which definitely put him within her personal space. And her into his personal space, come to think of it, although he maybe didn't mind so much as she minded…not that she minded. Not that she had much left of her mind at this point.

"No," he said, tipping up her chin with his hand. "I mean this."

Chessie's eyelids fluttered closed as he touched his mouth to hers. Which was probably a good thing, because then she didn't miss any of the colorful fireworks that immediately began bursting against them.

She hadn't been kissed in a long time. And she hadn't liked the kiss when it had happened. It had been one of those *I took you to dinner and a movie and now I expect payment* kind of kisses, courtesy of the last blind date Will had set her up with nearly eight months ago.

So of course this kiss was better. It didn't have to be much of a kiss at all to be better than her last.

Except this one was not only better than her last kiss, it won hands down over any she'd had in her entire life. Maybe three lifetimes.

His mouth tasted of sugared iced tea, and his tongue had probably gotten its Ph.D. in Persuasion, with a special commendation for Artful Insinuation.

She wanted to gulp him down, tear off his clothes, lick the sweat and salt from his muscled belly, dig her fingers into his shoulders so she could use them for leverage as she half vaulted him, scissored her legs around his back, pumped her eager lower body against him until he was so rock hard that she could feel him through his jeans.

And then she'd get *really* serious about seducing him….

As if he knew what she wanted, or maybe he wanted it, too, Jace cupped her backside in both of his strong hands and ground his lower body against hers. No words required. None were needed. They both knew what they wanted from each other.

This was desire. Lust. Raw need. Animal magnetism.

Good stuff. That's what it was.

Good stuff. Heady stuff. Can't-stop-it-now stuff. Who-cares-if-it's-right-or-wrong stuff. I-don't-need-to-know-your-name stuff. I don't even have to like you. You don't have to like me. I'm hungry; you're hungry. Let's eat.

Sex. It's what's for dinner….

Jace pulled his mouth away from hers, pressed his lips to her ear. "You're vibrating."

"Tell me something I don't know," Chessie all but gasped, trying to catch her breath, as she apparently hadn't been breathing there for a while. Was surprised she hadn't forgotten how. He didn't have to talk. She didn't need him to talk, preferred he didn't talk. She just *needed*. If he didn't watch out, she might just get there on her own, just from thinking about what she wanted him to do next. She'd never felt like this before in her life. She *liked* it!

His low chuckle helped bring her back to earth. "No, I mean something in your pocket. I think it's your cell phone."

Sanity knocked on the door to Chessie's libido, and her libido, so entirely unused to company, idiotically let it in.

"Oh. My cell phone. Right. It could be important. I should answer it, huh?"

Jace stepped away from her just as her knees threatened to buckle. "To be continued later?"

"Is…is that a question, or are you just being smug?"

"Do you care?"

Things like this didn't happen to people like her. Sexual innuendo. Raw, primitive lust. Openly acknowledging that, yes, she wanted to have sex with somebody. There was no dance, no courtship, no promises. No flattery or flowers. No agenda or destination other than getting him inside of her as deep as he could go and then watching his face as he drove into her again and again until they both exploded in a physical release that was the entire object of the game.

A sudden visual image stole her breath. Her caller could leave her a voice mail.

"I have a date tonight," she heard herself say. "A blind date. I can't get out of it. It…it's for a dinner party at my cousin's house. If I didn't show up, it would make the numbers uneven. And I think the only reason for the dinner party is to…"

Jace picked up the plans and his measuring tape and began backing toward the door to the hallway. Was he angry? Did he look angry? Did he have any right to be angry?

Chessie decided he wasn't angry. And then got a little angry that he wasn't angry.

Talk about your mixed-up heads—she ought to have hers examined the first chance she got!

"Set you up? Been there, done that."

"Got the T-shirt?"

"Didn't want one. I'm not into relationships."

"I didn't ask."

"I know."

"I'm divorced. I found my wife in bed with another man."

"I was left at the altar. He ran off with my maid of honor, and I doubt they'd only been sharing longing glances before they hopped that plane to Mexico. Which do you think is worse?"

He stepped back another pace, his eyes still very much locked with hers. "Are we keeping score?"

"I'm just saying. I'm not into relationships, either."

"Good. Because I don't want one."

"No. I know what you want. You made that pretty obvious."

"I didn't hear you telling me to stop."

Chessie pressed her crossed hands against her chest. "Oh, darling, are we having our first fight?"

Jace laughed, shook his head. "You're something else, Chessie Burton. Don't make me like you."

"I wouldn't think of it. Whatever was going on here had nothing to do with liking. We know nothing about each other. We should probably keep it that way."

"What was 'going on here'? Say it, Chessie. We were about to have sex, and if that phone hadn't vibrated we'd probably be done by now, because there wasn't going to be anything slow or easy about where we were heading."

Chessie felt another blush starting and turned her face away from his gaze. "Yes, I know. But you started it," she said, feeling like a child in a childish argument.

"Let's at least be honest here, Chessie. We both started it, the first time we saw each other. And it's not going to go away unless we finish it."

She turned to answer him, saying what, she didn't know. But the doorway was empty.

She dropped onto the bed, her chest rising and falling rapidly, as if she'd just run a marathon in some alternate universe, where she was a sex-starved nymph in transparent flowing draperies and he was the flesh-and-bone mating invention of some mad scientist out to re-populate the world with six-pack abs.

A vacation. That's what she needed. A long vacation far, far away from here. Long enough so that the addition would be done and he'd be gone by the time she got back. Because she could never face him again after this, and she was sure he wouldn't have the same problem. No, he'd just be there every day for the next three weeks or so; no shirt, big smile, crinkly creases around his eyes, and oozing sex from every pore. Just *there*, waiting for her to give him the signal.

Chessie sat up all at once. Signal? What was the signal? She didn't know any signals. She didn't even know who she was anymore, because she certainly wasn't the woman who had almost…almost— Good Lord!

"I'm not going to think about this anymore," she told herself as she stood in front of the mirror over the bathroom sink, reapplying her lipstick. "Everyone is entitled to one aberration in a lifetime. He was mine, but I was saved by the bell, and now I'm over it. It's out of my system. He's out of my system. He was never *in* my system. I don't even like him. He's arrogant, and assuming, and clearly just out for what he can get, and I—

"Good Lord. Now I'm trying to set myself up as either a victim or a Goody Two-shoes who didn't know what I was doing even as I was doing it. The man is sex on a stick. He can't help it. The only question is, do I take what he's offering, or do I do the sensible thing and walk away?"

Her reflection had no answer for her. Neither did her formerly rational brain nor her once-bruised and now wary heart.

But her body? Oh, her body had cast its vote before she'd even finished the question.

"Where'ya goin', Jace? Is something on fire somewhere?"

Jace had already picked up his lunch bucket and was heading toward the alley and his pickup when Carl asked his question. He turned back to look at the man, his mind racing to come up with a reason he was walking off the job. Okay, running off the job.

"I need to go downtown, check on some permits. I think we're going to enlarge Ms. Burton's existing bathroom, make it a Jack-and-Jill open to the workroom, which is going to change the entryway from the bedroom to the workroom, and I'm going to have to amend the plumbing permit to do that." As lies went, this was a pretty good one, and he decided he would do just that. He'd tell Marylou about it when he saw her. She'd approve it. She'd pretty much tossed the job at him and told him to do anything he wanted with it.

But she'd never told him much about Chessie Burton. Jace wished she had. Maybe then he wouldn't act like a complete ass every time he saw her.

"Okay, sounds good. But there's a problem. I just got

a call from Bob. He says that flatbed with the siding we were expecting today broke down on the turnpike. They're sending a new cab, but it will probably be six o'clock before it gets here. I called the wife, but she can't pick up Aiden, so I can't stay, and George—"

"It's okay, Carl. I'll be back in plenty of time, and I'll wait for the delivery. No problem. Gotta go."

Jace escaped the scene of the crime—okay, now that was being a little dramatic—and then drove to the nearby park and carried his lunch pail down to the stream and the waiting ducks.

A slice of bologna for him, a few hunks of bread for the ducks. A pickle for him, a slice of bologna for the ducks. His entire second sandwich, his small bag of potato chips and the container of green grapes for the ducks. The slice of bologna he had eaten, lying in his stomach like a chunk of cement.

What the hell had he done? What the hell had he been thinking?

Had he been thinking?

Hell, no. His hormones had been doing the thinking. Never a good idea. Never.

Damn, she'd tasted good. Tasted good, felt good, looked good.

He hadn't been able to get her out of his mind since that first morning. Three days. Three days he'd waited, wondering when he'd see her again. And nothing.

Then suddenly there she was, all smiles and iced tea and flushed cheeks and that way she had of sort of tipping her chin down and looking up at him through those in-credible long black lashes. Those huge blue eyes. Those see-into-her-soul blue eyes. Trying not to look, unable to look away. And that was both of them. She knew he couldn't stop looking at her, devouring her with his own eyes.

God, she was funny. Odd funny, silly funny, nervous funny.

Every moment they were in each other's company, you could cut the tension with the proverbial knife.

He'd honestly thought the kiss would do it. Cut the growing tension. Satisfy his curiosity. And hers.

Next time he had a bright idea he should go soak his head in something wet and cold until the feeling passed.

At least she'd come to her senses, even regained her sense of humor with that *darling* crack. And she'd turned down his arrogant suggestion that they meet again later, finish what they'd started. Nice to know he was attracted to a woman with a brain. *Not* nice to know he'd already decided he hated her blind date and hoped he got food poisoning at lunch and would have to call and cancel.

He wadded up the sandwich wrappings and shoved them back in his lunchbox before heading back up the hill toward the pickup, a couple of the ducks, hoping for dessert, he guessed, following him.

Tossing the lunchbox onto the front seat, Jace turned and leaned back against the driver's side door, trying to remember the last time he'd been so consumed by a woman, and finally decided the answer to that was *never*. Not even with Marci.

He wondered if Marci had known that, sensed it, acted as she had because of it. Because he hadn't been a good husband. He'd had his job during the day, college courses at night and then his fledgling business that took all of his energy and concentration…and devotion. He'd been 110 percent devoted to building his business. His marriage had been a casualty of his ambition.

So that was it; he wasn't marriage material. And he wasn't in a hurry to take another swing that would probably end up as strike two. Even being around Second Chance Bridal made him sort of knot up inside. How did Chessie stand it, having been left at the altar as she'd said she'd been? You'd think she would stay as far away from anything to do with weddings as possible.

Funny girl. Odd girl.

He couldn't get her out of his head. That, and the last thing he'd said to her. That asinine near challenge: *It's not going to go away unless we finish it.*

What a stupid macho thing to say.

"Who the hell does saying something like that make me?" he muttered to the world at large.

There was a strange, fairly strangled *quack* coming from ground level. Jace looked down to see that one of the larger ducks—a female, naturally—had just christened his right work boot with a suggested answer.

"I was thinking of it more as a rhetorical question," he said, smiling in spite of himself. "But thanks anyway...."

Chapter Three

"So tell me again how this happened, Chess," Marylou said as she dropped into a chair in the reception area of Second Chance Bridal just as Chessie entered from the hallway leading to the dressing rooms. "I thought you'd made it clear to Will that you weren't going on any more blind dates he set up for you."

"And hello to you, too. I didn't hear you come in." Chessie slipped the rhinestone tiara back into the glass case and locked it for the night. Katie Harwell had been right, the tiara had been too much, but selling her the cathedral-length train had sweetened the bottom line of the sale, so that was all right. "It wasn't Will this time. It was Elizabeth. I felt sort of stuck, you know?" She looked across the room at her friend and business partner and frowned. "Tell me you didn't get more collagen injected into your lips."

"All right," Marylou said, holding the cool aluminum of the soda can she'd just taken from the mini-fridge against her mouth. "I did not get more collagen injected into my lips."

Chessie opened the armoire that hid the minifridge and pulled out a diet cola for herself. "Liar, liar, French-cut pants on fire."

"Only as a matter of degree. You were being specific. You said collagen. I didn't have collagen injected into my lips. I had some of my very own fanny fat injected into the area just around my lips. So, *not* a liar. And the swelling will go down in a couple of days. Ted's in Vegas with some golfing buddies, and I'll be all happily pouty but not too swollen by the time he gets back."

Chessie subsided into the facing chair, sighing. "Marylou, you're a beautiful woman—"

"I'm a passably attractive fifty-five-year-old woman married to a forty-eight-year-old man who thinks I'm fifty-two. There, how's that for BFF-to-BFF honesty."

"Pretty good," Chessie said, nodding. "Except you're fifty-six. And," she said as Marylou tried to make a face—the fanny fat and some sort of injections to her forehead pretty much defeating that effort—"Ted loves you."

"Yes, third time's the charm. He knows I'm fifty-six. He still calls me his child bride. I think we're going to renew our vows next year, in Tahiti. Or maybe Rome.

We haven't decided. I never get tired of wearing wedding gowns. I'm thinking a lace sheath. Ecru, maybe with a colored sash. Now tell me again about this date. Is he someone local?"

Chessie realized she hadn't asked. In fact, all she knew about Toby Nieth was that he wasn't the country singer, Toby Keith, and she'd have to remember that or else she'd probably screw up at some point and ask him how his last tour went. "Elizabeth tells me he's a doctor."

"Really? Doctors are good. What kind?"

"I don't know. He's a doctor-doctor. It doesn't make a difference what kind of doctor he is."

"It would if he was a witch doctor," Marylou said quietly. "Anyway, I'm proud of you for doing this. I know how much you hate blind dates. That's why I've given up. No more matchmaking for me with you, Chess, I took the pledge. You're just not ever going to get married. It's very possible you're still carrying a torch for old what's-his-name."

"Rick?" Chessie was shocked. Nobody mentioned Rick to her. Not ever. She could joke about her aborted trip down the aisle, but that was her. For everyone else, the subject had been tacitly agreed to be out-of-bounds. "Why would you mention him? Why would you think that?"

Marylou's expression being cosmetically rendered unreadable, darn it, Chessie could only listen to the words, not watch for telltale signs of fibbing. Or con-niving. "Because he's back in town and you haven't said anything about that to me or to anyone, which might mean you're afraid of old feelings rising to the top and bubbling where everyone can see them. At least that's the general consensus."

Was there a Chessie's World website floating around the internet that she didn't know about? How did everyone know so much about her private life? Not that she *had* a private life. One private almost-tryst—did people still say *tryst?*—earlier this same day, but certainly not a private life. "How do you know Rick's back in town?"

Marylou got up and deposited the empty soda can in the recycle bin beneath the kidney-shaped registration desk. "I haf my vays," she said, doing an impression of Mata Hari, or some other spy with a bad German accent. "Not that I know much." She turned and sort of smiled at Chessie. "He's living at home with his mother—pitiful— his divorce from the bimbo maid of honor was final six months ago, he drives a three-year-old Mercedes—leased, and the cheaper model—and he's working as a junior broker at Gibbons, Fiorello and Schultz on Hamilton Boulevard. Oh, and he's got just the teensiest little bit of a sparse spot starting right at the crown of his head, for which he uses that liquid stuff you buy at the drugstore and rub on your head twice a day." She rolled her eyes. "Other than that, I know nothing."

"You never cease to amaze me, Marylou," Chessie said sincerely. "How do you know he's rubbing hair restorer on his head? Or don't I want to know?"

"You probably don't, although I will say the drugstore

at that new shopping center on Cedar Crest Boulevard has a very nice selection of eye shadows."

Chessie tried not to laugh, but it was difficult. "You've been *stalking* the man? How did you do it? Did you wear a trench coat with the collar pulled up? Or just dark sunglasses and a blond wig?"

Marylou rolled her eyes. "Don't be ridiculous. Let's just say I happened to be in the same place he was a few times in the past week or so. But I'm done with that. Just be glad he doesn't use that spray-on hair stuff some men use and think we don't notice. Run your hand through a guy's hair and come out with sticky gunk all over your fingertips and, believe me, *you know.*"

"Well, you and the rest of the world can relax. I'm not going to be running my fingers through Rick's hair, Marylou. He called here once, nearly two weeks ago, and I did not call him back. Clearly he took the hint. And I am not still carrying some torch for him. Rick Peters is filed away under Lucky Escape, and that's that. I just don't like being set up. There's something creepy about it. So thank you for not doing it anymore, and if you could convince everyone else, I'd be eternally grateful."

Marylou gave her a hug. "Honey, I've told them and *told* them. She doesn't want your help, I told them. She's happy as she is. *Alone.* But you know how happily marrieds can be. They want everyone else to be happily married, too."

Chessie disengaged herself from her friend's expensively scented embrace and held her at arm's length. "So you really did hire Jace Edwards because he came highly recommended? And not in some typical whacked-out Marylou Smith-Bitters idea of throwing him in front of me and vice versa?"

Marylou almost succeeded in making a face this time, she seemed that appalled. "Jace? Don't be ridiculous. He's not at all your type. You need a doctor, a dentist—heaven forbid, a stockbroker. Someone more…refined. He's a hunk, certainly, and seems nice enough. I'm sure I can find somebody for him if I just flashed his photo a few times, and since I've given up on you, he might make an interesting project. But not you, Chess, he's not at all right for you. He's much too *male*. Rough and tumble, self-made, a little too earthy around the edges."

"Too *male* for me? Are you saying Jace Edwards is too much *man* for me? That I'm not enough *woman* for him?"

"No, sweetheart, of course not." Marylou crooned sweetly as she gave Chessie another little hug, and then patted her cheek.

Chessie wouldn't have called either the hug or the face-pat patronizing…but only because she couldn't seem to find her own voice.

"I'm only saying that you're, well, you're not very sensually minded."

"Says who?" Chessie said at last, her voice sounding just a little squeaky. "I am so sensually minded. I think. What does that mean? I mean, to you, Marylou. To me, it sounds like you think I'm a cold fish. Without…needs.

I've got…you know. *Needs.* And before you pat my cheek again, you might want to rethink the gesture."

Marylou raised her hands to show she was harmless. "The fact that you have to ask me what it means to be sensually minded is probably your first clue here, Chessie. Look, let's conduct a small poll, all right?"

"Are you going to publish the results? Because I have a feeling my life is being discussed when I'm not there."

"You have friends, Chess. Friends who love you. Everything we do, we do out of love. There," she ended briskly. "Happy now? Good. Back to the poll. First question—have you ever had casual sex?"

Chessie didn't answer her.

"Part two of that question while you're thinking over part one—have you ever had a one-night stand?"

"It used to be a virtue to not sleep around, you know," Chessie said, wondering why she was feeling so defensive.

"So that's a no and a no. Question two—how bad a lover was this Rick Peters, anyway?"

Chessie thought her eyes might pop out of her head. "What? What does that have to do with anything?"

Marylou seemed to want to hug her again, so Chessie stepped back, out of reach.

Her friend looked toward the armoire. "We don't have any wine in there, do we? We really should rethink that. All right, what does your ex-fiancé's prowess as a lover or lack thereof have to do with it? I'd have to say everything, wouldn't I? And there's been no one else since him? Not in six years?"

Chessie lowered her head, rubbing two fingers against the tense wrinkles forming between her eyebrows. She was going to be a candidate for fanny-fat injections herself if this kept up. "Two. There were two, all right? But no one-night stands, no casual sex for sex's sake. At least I don't think they were."

"Two men in six years." Marylou sighed, blinking rapidly, as if fighting tears. "I've heard about women who can take it or leave it. I didn't really believe you were one of them until lately, but sweetheart, facts are facts. You've got this place, the romance without the passion, and you like it that way. You're an...observer, not really a participant. And that's all right, sweetheart. Really it is. You simply aren't—sensually minded. I mean, I'd like to say you're simply unawakened, and Prince Charming will come riding in on his great white horse and wake you up to what you're missing, but I don't think so."

"I could, too, just be unawakened," Chessie said hopefully, thinking back to the events in her bedroom earlier today. "I could be just about ready to pop, actually."

"You say that as if you want me to go back to matchmaking for you."

"No! No, I'm not saying that. God, no, I've already seen your work when it comes to me. I'm just saying that maybe you're wrong. Maybe...maybe this guy tonight will be the one. He could be. Because I'm not still hung up on Rick. That is *so* not true. I've just been working a lot, establishing my business, and I'm working hard again now that we're partners. That doesn't mean I don't have…don't have needs. For all you know, I could be planning on having mad monkey sex tonight! Wild, crazy, unbridled sex with…with a complete stranger!"

"Knock, knock" came a male voice from somewhere behind her. "I guess I'm interrupting something? Girl talk?"

"Oh, *God*," Chessie groaned, longing to disappear into the floor. Did he hear anything? Of course he'd heard something. For all she knew, he could have been standing behind the door, taking notes. "What do *you* want?"

Jace Edwards stepped into the room, immediately clogging it with testosterone. "Well, it's probably a little late to wish I could have been deaf for the last couple seconds, Ms. Burton, so I guess I'll settle for asking you for the keys to your side door. One of our circular saws took a walk last night, so I want to lock up the tools in your basement until the addition is far enough along to secure it. If that's all right with you?"

"Yeah. Right. Uh-huh, sure, I'll…I'll go get you one." Chessie kept her head down as she brushed past him and headed for her office. Where she would curl up in a ball and simply die, because it was easier than ever having to face that man again.

"Bye, Chessie," Marylou called after her. "Good luck on your date tonight."

No! Don't leave me don't leave me don't— Oh, hell. Chessie flinched when she heard the bell tingle as the front door of the shop closed. Rats deserted sinking ships with less speed.

"Found one?" Jace asked from the doorway.

She kept her back to him. And since she was standing in the middle of her office, several steps away from her desk or anything else that might hold a key, she thought the answer was obvious. "I haven't looked yet. I was busy mentally composing a new last will and testament before going upstairs and sticking my head in the oven. I'm cutting out Marylou, by the way. You might want to warn her."

"I didn't hear much," Jace said, his voice closer now, so that she hastened over to the desk and began pulling out drawers, looking inside them but really not seeing anything. "Just the monkey-sex part. I never understood that. What do monkeys know that we don't? Aren't we supposed to be the evolved ones? Maybe someday we can go to Philly to the zoo, and see if it's all it's cracked up to be. Do you suppose the Monkey House is rated R, or do they let just anybody in?"

Her hand closed on a ring of keys and she yanked one off and held it out in his direction. "Here. Take it. Go. You were supposed to be gone an hour ago."

"Late delivery. You were supposed to have a date. But hey, there's still time to cancel it if you'd like to grab a burger with me."

"Thanks, but no thanks," she said, finally turning to look at him, which was a mistake. He'd changed his clothes. Instead of jeans and a loose button shirt and work boots, he was wearing jeans and sneakers and a black T-shirt that could have been painted on for all she knew.

Black shirt, black hair, gray eyes, a great tan, a bit of a five-o'clock shadow and all those muscles. There wasn't anything *GQ* about Jace Edwards. Nothing slick or smooth. If he was going to pose for anything it would be for the cover of one of those romance novels where the guy is all bare-chested and standing with his legs braced apart and the girl is half-naked on her knees in front of him, touching his abs and looking up at him as if she wanted to start a hands-on inventory from where she was, working her inquisitive fingers to all his most interesting places before—

"After you lock up, drop the keys through the mail slot. I'll give them to you again in the morning."

"I am bonded," he told her in some amusement. "And I don't think I'd look too good in any of those gowns back there anyway. But, okay. I'll take the key in the morning, slip it through the mail slot every night. Chessie? Are you sure you're all right?"

The disturbing mental image of Jace as virile romance hero and her as eager virgin in a low-cut gown and all but begging to be tossed to the ground and ravished in wild and sundry ways went *pop* and disappeared. She'd added a dashing eye patch just moments earlier, and a pirate sword at his belt. They'd both been nice touches, she'd thought. She should have lost the eye patch and added a gag....

"Of course I'm all right. I'm always all right. I make it a point to be all right. Why wouldn't I be all right? Oh—would you please just *go away?*"

"I like you in that color," he said, just as she was seriously considering braining him with the stapler. "What's it called?"

"Pink. It's called pink." The bell over the front door tinkled in warning. "Oh, damn it, he's here."

"Just what a man wants to hear when he's showing up for his first date with a woman. Encouraging as all hell," Jace said, chuckling. "Why don't you go get yourself a glass of cold water or something. I'll keep him company until you get back."

"Don't you dare go out there and—"

But he was already gone. And he was probably right. She did need a few moments to compose herself before meeting Toby Keith—*Nieth*. Before meeting Toby *Nieth*.

She snuck out of the office and took the stairs two at a time, heading for her kitchen and the pitcher of ice water she kept in the refrigerator. She didn't have a headache, but took two aspirin anyway, just because someone as upset as she was at the moment couldn't be counted on not to have a coronary or something and aspirin was supposedly good for that.

Then, realizing she'd just left her date and her whatever-he-was downstairs together, she bounded down the steps once more, smoothed down her skirt, ran her fingers through her hair, moistened her lips with the tip of her tongue, put a smile on her face and walked toward the lion's den…er, the reception area.

She saw Toby Nieth before he saw her, so she took that moment to look him over, see what it was Elizabeth seemed to think would appeal to her. And didn't find much. He was tall, although not as tall as Jace. He was slender but also looked fit, as if maybe he ran or cycled for exercise. She wondered if he shaved his legs. She'd known a bicyclist once who shaved his legs, said it cut down on wind drag or something. That had been a fast one-date thing. She just couldn't get past the mental image of a guy sitting on the edge of the tub, lathering up his legs and taking a razor to them.

Back to Toby Nieth.

His hair was sort of sandy and maybe a little too short around the ears, a little too stylishly long on top. He wore tan leather loafers, no socks, khaki slacks with knife-sharp creases, a dark green open-neck golf shirt, and had a white sweater edged in green over his shoulders, the sleeves tied in a knot over his chest.

Tennis, anyone? The expression entered her head and she banished it just as quickly as it had come. This was what Elizabeth saw as a good match for her? Toby Nieth seemed so contrived, so what-the-well-dressed-young-executive-should-look-like. So fake.

But probably safe, which would have been Marylou's comment if she were here and thank God she wasn't. Nonthreatening. Not so overwhelmingly *male*.

Like some people Chessie didn't want to mention and

wished on the other side of the universe right now. And what was he doing? Handing Toby a can of soda and offering him a chair? As if he was some kind of *host* or something? Oh no. Oh, no, no, no. *Don't you go sitting down, Jace Edwards, not unless you want me to dump you out of that chair on your head!*

"Hi!" she said just a smidgen too enthusiastically as she walked into the reception area, her right hand outstretched as both men got to their feet once more, "I'm so sorry I'm late. I'm Chessie. And you must be—"

"Toby Nieth, Ms. Chessie Burton," Jace interrupted. "And she really is sorry. I told her earlier. I said, Chess, honey, we really have to stop talking and get you ready for your date. But you know how women are."

Chessie's eyes popped open wide. He made it sound as if he'd been sitting on her bed or something while she got dressed for her date. And how women are what? But she didn't ask, because he'd probably have an answer.

"Yes," she said instead. "Jace here is putting a little addition on the back of the building for us. Nothing too difficult, as we don't want to strain his intellect, or spread his limited talents too thinly. But he's coming along, and we're always happy to help a struggling entrepreneur. Still taking those classes, aren't you, Jace? One day you might be able to say you're a real honest-to-goodness plumber. Your mother will be so proud."

Toby Nieth spoke for the first time. "I thought you said you owned your own construction company," he said, looking at Jace.

Whose ears were such a nice shade of red at the moment. Ha!

"Chess likes to tease. Don't you, Chess," Jace said with his back to Toby, smiling at her in a way that probably would look good on a serial killer. "Before you go, I do have a question about the new storage room. Do you want a separate thermostat in there? Because it might be a good idea to *cool it down* a little."

"Really? I didn't think it was all that hot in the first place."

"Chessie?" Toby said, looking like a man who'd just walked in on the second act and hadn't been told any of his lines. "Look, uh, I parked my Benz in the loading zone out front, so how about I go out there and keep watch, and you join me when you're ready."

She nodded and then promised she'd only be a minute.

The moment the door was closed, she turned to Jace in a fury. "What is the *matter* with you? What did you think you were doing?"

"You're not going to have hot monkey sex with that plastic jerk tonight," he said flatly.

"Oh, I'm not? How do you know? And it was mad monkey sex, not hot monkey sex."

"There's a difference? We really need to take that trip to the zoo during mating season. Or, you know, maybe we could catch something on one of those nature channels."

"Would…you…shut…*up!*"

"He's wearing his sweater over his shoulders and tied in a knot. You caught that, right? You two going to dinner, or a tennis match? And he'll be waiting by his Benz, Chessie. You ought to count tonight, see how many different brand names he can drop into the conversation. I've already heard about the Benz and the Rolex, and I'd only been talking to him—okay, listening to him—for five minutes. Next up, I'm thinking, will be the two glorious weeks he spent in Machu Pichu."

"He's been to Machu Pichu? Oh, never mind, you're just making that up. And what do you care?"

"I don't know, and you're right, I don't care. And I'm being honest here. Not totally honest, because I heard more earlier than I'd like you to know I did. About you being, you know, repressed sexually? I just don't feel comfortable thinking I might have wound you up just to have you let it go with that guy."

Chessie felt herself make a face rather like a high-speed animation of a prune turning into a raisin; probably not her best look. "Wound me up? You—if you don't have the biggest head in the known world. Wound me *up?* What? And now you're worried maybe you've unleashed a sex-starved monster into that world? Well, hell, Jace, don't just stand there. Run outside and warn poor Toby Keith away, why don't you?"

"Nieth. Toby *Nieth,*" Jace corrected maddeningly, exasperatingly. "If you're going to go to bed with the guy, you really should know his name. But you won't like it, Chess."

"Yes, I know," she said, her voice dripping sarcasm.

"One lousy kiss, and you've spoiled me for all other men. In your dreams, Jace Edwards, in your dreams, which is the only place I'll *ever* be with you." She grabbed up her purse and slung the strap over her shoulder. "You just remember to put the key through the mail slot when you're done."

She stormed out of the salon and down the walk, stopping when she saw Toby Neith striking a clearly planned and not nonchalant pose against the Benz, his bare ankles crossed just so as he readjusted the knot in his sweater sleeves. Was Elizabeth out of her mind?

Maybe they all thought she was sensuality deprived. Maybe they were just all tired of setting the table for five instead of six, seven instead of eight. Maybe they thought she could only relate to men as harmless as Elizabeth was probably sure Toby Nieth was. And, Chessie had learned, it was always the safe-looking ones, the polite ones, that turned into eight-handed octopusses—octopi?—once they got you home again.

Or maybe they were all afraid she'd jump at the chance to be with Rick again.

Did none of her friends really know her?

Chessie looked back up the walkway toward the salon. Given the choice of a pleasant evening with Will and Elizabeth and another maddening confrontation with the totally unacceptable and maybe even unlikable but definitely sexy Jace Edwards, she knew which one she'd choose. In a heartbeat.

Which begged the question: Did she even know herself?

* * *

Three hours later, Jace heard the Benz pull away from the curb, and grinned the sort of grin that could get him in big trouble if anyone else saw it. Poor Tennis Anyone Toby. The guy was going to need new tires if he kept laying rubber like that.

He got up off his knees, sliding the hammer back into his tool belt, walked to the entrance to the reception area, and waited for the sound of Chessie's key in the front door. The slam of that same door brought another wicked smile to his lips.

He casually flipped the light switch next to him, turning on the overhead chandelier. "You're home early. Let me guess, your evening didn't go all that swimmingly?"

Chessie let out a small yelp of alarm that quickly turned into a "What the hell are you still doing here?" explosion of what might have been a touch of anger (a pretty big touch, almost a physical shove of anger, actually). "It's ten o'clock."

"Yes, and you left here at seven. Three hours. Factoring in travel time both ways, drinks before dinner, and that was a pretty quick evening. Did you decide to skip dessert?"

Chessie slipped off her high-heeled sandals, seemed to consider tossing one of them at him, but then put them down on top of one of the display cases. "Not funny, Jace. I repeat—what are you still doing here?"

"Puttering. You told me to put the key through the mail slot when I was done hauling the tools down to the basement. I did that. You never told me to close the door first. Or to leave."

"Next time I'll be more specific. But for future reference, you were supposed to leave."

He was driving her crazy. But she seemed to like it. He'd seen her smile before she could hide it. "I had nowhere to go. I'd eaten an early dinner, the Phillies are traveling on the West Coast so they won't even be on TV until ten-thirty, and I had nothing else to do. Unlike you, with your busy social life."

She surprised him with her next question. "Are you sure? I thought they came on at ten."

"Late start. You like baseball?"

She picked up her shoes. "We're not having a conversation here, Jace. I was only making a comment. What do you mean? Puttering?"

He followed her toward the stairs, since she'd asked a question and it wouldn't do either of them much good for him to answer it with him downstairs and her up in her apartment. He'd like to think of it as an invitation to join her, but asking if she had any beer in the fridge would probably be overdoing it.

"Puttering is pretty much what it sounds like. When I took the tools down to the basement, I noticed that you had some dripping going on from the faucet in the laundry tub. I put in new washers, and then decided to check the rest of the faucets in the house as long as I had my handy-dandy wrench out anyway."

She stopped at the top of the stairs to turn her head

and look at him, rolling those great big baby-blue eyes at him. "Handy-dandy wrench?"

"That's what we apprentice plumbers call it," he said to her back, as she was on the move again. "And by the way, my mother is still having trouble accepting that I'm a contractor. She'd hoped for another lawyer in the family. Except when she's calling me to come over and fix something, that is, because my father the lawyer couldn't screw in a lightbulb without a consultation with three other lawyers and a written brief on clockwise-versus-counter-clockwise."

"Now *that's* funny," she tossed back at him. "I'm listening. Keep going."

"Yes, ma'am," he said, longing to give that pert backside of hers a playful slap. "You didn't need any more washers, but the door to your bathroom was really out of plumb—old houses settle, and what hung straight in the nineteen hundreds can go crooked. You're lucky you never got stuck inside the bathroom. Or outside of it. I don't know which would be worse."

Chessie tossed her shoes and purse on an overstuffed chair and headed for the kitchen. "I suppose you want coffee?"

He followed yet again, and then leaned one shoulder against the door jamb, admiring the view. "The gracious hostess. Yes, thank you. Please notice that there's now a cover on that outlet. Do you have any idea how dangerous it is to not have a cover on an outlet? Especially a kitchen outlet?"

"The old one cracked a few weeks ago, probably from old age. I was meaning to buy a new one," she said as she filled the coffeepot at the sink. "Okay, so we've established what puttering is. Unsolicited puttering, mind you, so don't try adding it to the bill. Anything else?"

"Your lingerie drawer sticks."

She swung around so quickly, a heavy earthenware coffee cup in her hand, that she nearly took out the pot of African violets on the windowsill. "That's *not* funny," she said once she realized he had been joking.

"I don't know, Chess. I liked it. You came into the shop as if you couldn't wait to slam the door behind you, and on Tennis Anyone, and then he peeled out of here in his *Benz* as if somebody was chasing him. Was your date really that much of a bust?" *I hope, I hope.*

"It wasn't that bad," she said, turning back to the counter. "Will and Elizabeth are always good company, and she made her special chicken-and-rice dish I really like. There was plenty of conversation. Fourteen," she ended, sounding more relaxed, even amused.

"Fourteen what— Wait, I get it now." Jace took the coffee cup she offered, shaking his head to the offer of cream or sugar. "Fourteen brand-name mentions. Damn. I think I had an even dozen in the pool."

"Well, some of them were repeats, although I counted each one, and other people had to have some time to talk, and I wasn't with him that long. Still, it comes out to more than four every sixty minutes. Sort of like commercials on TV."

"Except you couldn't pick up your remote and change the channel until they were over."

She followed him back into the living room. "Good point. We didn't really hit it off from the get-go, no thanks to you. He made a move on me anyway, probably just because he thought I'd expect one."

Jace put his coffee cup down on the table beside his chair. Probably a little too hard. "That bare-ankled bastard."

Chess took up a spot on the couch, pulling her bare legs up next to her on the cushion, making Jace immediately rethink his stupid decision to sit in a chair.

"Why so surprised, Jace? You made a move on me. So obviously it's not like you think I'm un-move-on-able material."

"He didn't even know you."

"Oh? And you do? Three days of you outside making way too much noise and me inside wishing you'd go away does not make for a great acquaintance."

"I'll ignore that. What kind of move?"

Chess took a sip of coffee. Or pretended to, so she could hide her smile, which Jace saw anyway. "What do you mean, what kind of move? He drove me home, we sat out front in his Benz while I thanked him for a lovely evening, I didn't want him to walk me to the door so I sort of leaned over a little so he could kiss me good-night—that seemed only fair—and he made a move on me."

Jace wanted to hunt down Toby Nieth and seriously

rearrange his sweater sleeves so that the knot was in much closer proximity to his Adam's apple. He didn't know why he was having this reaction, and really didn't want to delve too deeply into that *why,* but right about now Toby Nieth should be considering himself a very lucky man that he hadn't pulled his stunt inside Second Chance Bridal.

"Okay. So what did *you* do?"

"Oh, no. If I tell, then I wouldn't be able to use my trusted countermove on you if you ever tried anything."

"I tried something this afternoon," he reminded her, getting up from the chair and redepositing himself beside her on the couch. "I just might be about to try something again now."

"No, you aren't. You're smarter than that."

"I am?" Jace raised his eyebrows in surprise. He really did plan to kiss her. Wanted to kiss her. More and more needed to kiss her, if just to see if what happened that afternoon had been a fluke, and he wouldn't have that same gut-clenching reaction with a second kiss. "Why am I smarter than that?"

She laid her head back against the cushions and sighed. "One, you can tell that I'm upset by what happened with Toby. Two, you wouldn't want to be seen as taking advantage of me in my fragile condition. Three, you're giving me time to get to know you, and for you to get to know me, so that we both don't make a mistake at least one of us will regret. And four, I'm holding a cup of really hot coffee three inches above your crotch."

Jace, who had been otherwise engaged, visually taking in her profile, the sweep of her neck, picking out his initial point of approach, quickly looked down toward his lap. "You make a compelling argument," he said, careful not to move.

Her laugh was warm, throaty, and he actually sighed in relief as she sat forward once more and placed the cup on the coffee table. "I thought you might see it my way. Now, are you going home, or do we talk? I'm really not sleepy, and the coffee isn't decaf, so it's either you or the Phillies and the Dodgers."

"How about both?" Jace reached across her body, careful to keep his hand visible and nonthreatening, and picked up the TV remote before easing back to his previous position. "So you really are a Phillies fan?"

"I have season tickets to the Iron Pigs, if that answers your question. Third baseline, but up under cover, because I'm not enough of a fan to have to worry about foul balls and errant bats that might go flying in my direction. I like seeing players who might make it to the big show, and the ones who come down here for rehab before going back into the regular lineup."

"Interesting. How about football?"

She rolled those big blue eyes as if his question had been just too obvious for words. "Eagles fan. Isn't everyone? Now I've got one for you. Chocolate chip or peanut butter? Cookies," she added when he shook his head. "I've got both in the kitchen, and both homemade. Not by me, understand, but homemade. Which do you like?"

"Only a cruel and sadistic woman would ask a man to choose between chocolate chip and peanut butter. Although I'd like to trade in this coffee for a glass of milk. For dunking."

"Dipping," she told him very seriously. "One dunks a donut. One dips a cookie."

"Sorry. Didn't know I was dealing with an expert," he said, helping her to her feet before picking up both coffee cups and, once again, following where she led. It got easier and easier, following where Chessie Burton led.

Should he point out that a quick left turn would get them to her bedroom?

Probably not.

She wanted to get to know him, he'd let her get to know him. And, in turn, he would get to know her.

Then they could make that left turn into the bedroom.

Because some things couldn't be avoided. Not for long, anyway.

Chapter Four

"Stop that."

Chessie continued zipping up the gown she'd just re-placed on its hanger. "It's all right, Marylou, I don't mind. I know Missy is supposed to clean out the dressing rooms, but she's still at lunch and I don't have anything else to do."

"Not the cleaning up. You can keep going on that. I'm talking about the humming. The humming has to stop. Or at least pick another tune. As it is, I'll be hearing the lyrics in my head for the rest of the day anyway. 'I saw you and the world went'—somewhere."

"Away," Chessie supplied as she carefully zipped up the protective bag, not wanting to snare any of the lace on the gown's bodice. "The song is called 'Tonight.' 'Somewhere' is a different song."

"And they're both from the same show. But I can't remember what show they're from."

"West Side Story," Chessie supplied helpfully. "I watched it last night, or this morning I guess I should say, since it wasn't over until almost four. It never ends happily, yet I keep watching, hoping for something glorious to happen. This time I just turned it off before the last scene. There, that's the last of them."

Marylou took the gown and held it up high by the hanger as Chessie grabbed three others and they headed for the stockroom. "You didn't get to bed until four o'clock, and you're humming this morning? So the blind date went a lot better than I thought it would?"

Chessie opened her mouth to tell her friend about Jace, how he'd been there when she got home, how they'd sat over cookies and milk and talked for hours. About how he'd kissed her good-night, and she'd wanted him to do more than that, but he didn't, but that the promise was there. She'd felt that; and tonight was probably going to be the same as last night, but also so much more.

That promise had been in his eyes when he'd looked down at her as if she was somehow precious to him. Important. The promise was in his touch, the way he'd held her, but hadn't tried to possess her. In the kiss itself, which was sweet, yet tinged with a whisper of passion.

Oh, he was good. He was so good.

And she was so weak…

"Toby was really nice," she heard herself say instead. "We had a really good time."

"Really? You really had a *really* good time? Huh," Marylou said, looking confused. "Well, um…that's nice."

Tell a lie and it leads to more lies. Chessie heard the warning in her head, but she couldn't help herself. All her friends, but most especially Marylou, had been trying for years to match her up with someone. But this time she'd found someone all on her own, and she wasn't ready to share. It was too new, this feeling she had. Talking about it, about this *thing* she had with Jace might take some of the bloom off, while at the same time putting too much pressure on her.

Jace was her secret right now. She liked it that way. She was so weary of being told she had to think about her future. Right now she wanted to think about the present, or at least no more than eight or ten hours into the future. She was a grown-up, she was allowed to have…needs.

"Oh, yes. We didn't do so well over dinner," she said, not having to fake her blush at her fib, "so I'm guessing Elizabeth, if she reports in to you—"

"Elizabeth doesn't *report in* to me," Marylou objected.

"Sure she does. You all report to each other. Get Chessie a blind date and then have a strategy meeting afterward. Did she like him? Did he like her? The lawyer with the horn-rimmed glasses didn't make the cut. Okay, so maybe next time we'll try a dentist who plays golf?"

Marylou grinned that Cheshire Cat grin of hers that could mean anything—and usually did. "You make us all sound so conniving. We've only got your best interests at heart."

Chessie gave her friend a quick hug. "I know you do. And, hey, look how it's working out this time. You know, like hey, the forty-seventh time just might be the charm! Just please don't tell Elizabeth and Will. Or anyone. Let's just see where…where Toby and I go on our own."

"You won't even share with me?"

Chessie was getting into this now. "Nope. Not even with you. If I'm going to have a love life, I think I want to keep it to myself, at least for a while."

"A love life?" If she'd been the Wicked Witch of the West, Marylou would probably be cackling and rubbing her hands together by now, but she managed to abstain. More than managed to abstain. In fact, although it seemed impossible to believe, Marylou was actually looking a little disappointed. Maybe because Toby hadn't been her "find," but Elizabeth's.

"Well, maybe love life is a little strong," Chessie said. "But certainly a sex life."

Marylou's eyes, expression-erasing injections or not, went wide at that one. "Are you sure? I mean, you don't want to *rush* into anything."

"If I went any slower, Marylou, I might forget the moves. What's the matter? I thought you'd be happy."

"And I am—I am," Marylou said quickly. "And this has nothing to do with Rick Peters being back in town? I mean, you aren't just overreacting in some way, wanting to have somebody because it's safer than thinking about running into the one that got away?"

Darn it. Chessie hadn't thought about Rick a single time in the past twenty-four hours. Not that she'd thought of him all that much before then. But she had thought about him when she'd found out about his return to Allentown. Probably only because he'd been the one to do the leaving. It was easier to be the one that left than the one who got left. Left at the altar, no less.

She'd always thought it would be wonderful if he came crawling back, so then she could be the one who did the leaving. That would have given her closure on what had been a fairly terrible time in her life. After all, it wasn't every woman who got to stand in her bedroom in her wedding gown an hour before her wedding and be handed a note that pretty much said, "Sorry, but I've made other plans."

And not just Rick, but her supposed best friend, as well. How could she have been so wrong about what she believed to be the two best people in her life?

Rick and Diana had done a real number on Chessie's self-confidence, her ability to trust, her confidence in her own judgment. It was, she'd thought more than once, like being robbed. It took a long time before you felt safe again, able to trust.

She'd spent a lot of time—a *lot* of time—wondering what she'd done wrong, where she'd come up short, how she'd been so blind. But then, eventually, she'd picked herself up, dusted herself off, opened her business and sold her bridal gown to a woman who still stopped by once in a while to thank Chessie for making her second wedding so wonderful. She even brought her four-year-old twins with her, which was nice.

And Leanna had been only the first of what were now hundreds of happy second-chance brides that had passed through Chessie's life.

So something good had come from something bad. Chessie's entire career, this wonderful Victorian house, her friendships with Marylou and Elizabeth and Claire and so many others—all had come from Rick's defection.

And now, at long last, there was Jace. A man who excited her. A man who seemed to think she was desirable. A man who made her laugh, and get angry, and think about herself as someone who wasn't lacking, wasn't second-best.

Or did she just think that because Rick was back in town and she really, really needed to feel that way?

"Chessie?"

"Hmm?" she said, still lost in her thoughts.

"I'm sorry, sweetheart," Marylou said. "You were looking so happy, and then I brought up Rick's name. I shouldn't have done that."

"No, it's all right. Do you think I should have said yes to that invitation to dinner?"

"I don't know, Chess. What do you think?"

Chessie rolled her eyes. "Isn't that how psychologists

answer questions? What do *you* think? I don't know what I think, Marylou. That's why I'm asking you."

Marylou sighed. "Yes, I was afraid of that. Why don't you give it a few more days? Get to know— Toby's his name, right? Get to know Toby better. And then make a decision."

The sound of hammering began outside the stockroom, signaling the end of the crew's lunch break, and Chessie had to fight the impulse to go running outside to say hello, or do something equally obvious and stupid. "All right. I'll give it a few days. Get to know—" she gave a quick cough, having almost slipped and said Jace's name "—get to know Toby better. I'm certainly smart enough to be able to judge the difference between real feelings and, um, you know."

"Wild, unbridled lust?" Marylou suggested smoothly.

"Yeah," Chessie said, thinking about what had happened—almost happened—yesterday. What had a very good chance of happening tonight. "That."

Elizabeth put a protective hand to her baby belly as she slipped into the diner booth beside Claire, and the two of them looked across the table expectantly at Marylou.

"I really don't get it," Elizabeth said without preamble, as they'd all three had a conference call going an hour earlier, when Marylou had set up this strategy meeting. "It certainly didn't look to either Will or me that the two of them were going to be more than a single date. They have nothing in common. But I was desperate, and Toby was the only unattached male I could think of who we hadn't already set up with Chessie." She ripped open her straw and stuck it in the lemonade Marylou had ordered for her. "I'm not very good at this. I wish I were, because if it weren't for Chessie, Will and I would have never met. She deserves better than my paltry expertise."

Claire, still wearing her white medical coat, her stethoscope stuck in her pocket—they'd met at the diner next to the medical building where she worked as a physician's assistant in her brother's pediatric office—patted Elizabeth's arm. "Don't feel so bad. Remember Zane Fletcher? He was my last matchmaking effort. I just heard he's been disbarred for stealing money from his client's accounts. Besides, Marylou said Chessie likes your guy."

"No," Marylou corrected, "I said *Chessie* says she likes this guy. She also said I wasn't to say anything to Elizabeth, because she and this Toby guy didn't seem to hit it off at dinner, but only discovered that they liked each other after they left to go home. Now tell me neither of you smell something fishy about that."

Elizabeth sat back against the pseudoleather booth. "It would have had to have been a small miracle. I mean, it was a really awkward evening. Toby seemed to be as glad when it was over as Chessie did. Will says I'm barred from ever fixing up Chessie again, Bride Plan or no Bride Plan."

Claire looked at her watch. "I've got to get back to the office in a few minutes, so let's cut to the chase, all right?

What you're saying, Marylou, is that you think Chessie is lying to you about this Toby guy. Why would she do that?"

Marylou leaned in closer, so that the other two women did, as well. "I hate to say this. I mean, I really, really hate to say this. But I think she's seeing Rick Peters."

"Why does that name sound familiar?"

"He's her ex-fiancé," Elizabeth told Claire, who then nodded, made a sort of *uh-oh* sound in her throat. "But doesn't she hate him, Marylou? I'd hate him."

"So would I. *Detest* might be a better word."

"But neither of you are Chessie," Marylou pointed out, pushing away the paper napkin she'd been nervously shredding. "She didn't ask me if I agreed that she shouldn't have accepted Rick's invitation to dinner. She asked me if I thought she should have said yes. Like, maybe she was looking for some sort of justification for having already accepted Rick's invitation to dinner. I think that's what's happening tonight, and she's using this Toby guy as cover. I think she's really meeting with Rick."

"Maybe just to talk?" Elizabeth suggested weakly.

"She was *humming,* Elizabeth. Happy humming."

"Oh."

"I'd stake out the shop tonight and follow her if she goes out. Except that would be really disloyal."

"Not to mention bordering on creepy," Elizabeth said, smothering a grin.

"I know. Besides, Ted comes home tonight, so I'll be busy anyway. I'm just so worried about her."

"It is her life, Marylou," Claire pointed out, once more looking at her watch. "Although I do feel badly that she's hiding this from us. I guess she knows we wouldn't approve. Still, what can we do? We can't confront her. She's not a child. Speaking of which, I'm due back to do an intake on a new patient. Gotta go. You two tell me what you decide, and whatever it is, pretend I've already agreed, no matter how off-the-wall it might be. You know I'd do anything for Chessie."

Marylou put out a hand to stop them as Elizabeth went to slide from the booth to allow Claire to get out. "Just a second, Claire. Did you find somebody?" she asked her.

Claire motioned for Elizabeth to keep on moving. "Yes. A new doctor just took over the empty office suite on the third floor. Cardiologist. Nice guy, too. But if Chessie's seeing her ex-fiancé, does that really matter? Oh, wait, I get it. You want us to keep tossing choices in her direction, keep The Bride Plan going. All right, I'll set it up. But if she says no, there's really nothing I can do about that. I'll let you know."

Once Claire was gone, Elizabeth looked across the table at Marylou. "You're really worried, aren't you?"

"I thought I'd finally found the— Well, it doesn't matter what I thought, does it, since it didn't work. I really, really thought it would work. Mostly, I hate that Chessie feels she has to lie to me. To us. That has to mean that she knows seeing Rick Peters again is wrong." She sighed, and then wiped a tear from her eye with the part of the paper napkin she hadn't shredded. "Maybe she'll see him tonight and, well, do what she feels she needs to do, and then he'll be out of her system."

"The way you say that, Marylou, I could think that Chessie is planning to have sex tonight. Isn't that a stretch, even for you?"

Marylou sniffed, shook her head. "No, I know the signs. It's…it's like senior-prom night in that shop today. She's just wishing away the day so she can get to tonight and, you know—*graduate*."

Elizabeth laughed. "Are you saying that all girls have sex after their senior prom?"

Marylou looked confused. "You didn't?"

"Well, yes, but Jamie and I had been dating for a lot of years. It wasn't as if we hadn't—but that night was sort of special. So I guess I see what you mean. Seeing someone you loved enough to want to marry after six years of not seeing him could be thought of as sort of special. But for every girl who had a special night that night, there had to be an equal number who ended up really disappointed with the experience."

"Then we can only hope the real thing doesn't live up to the expectation," Marylou said as she reached for her glass of diet soda. "Because if Chessie looked any more expectant today, she'd look like you."

"Speaking of expectant me," Elizabeth said, waving to the waitress. "I spied out what looks to be some scrumptious strawberry pie in the case as I walked in here. Would you mind?"

"If we can get whipped cream with it, absolutely not. I may just eat myself into a stupor, so that I don't have to keep thinking about what might happen tonight."

They installed the last window ten minutes before five, and Jace had a set of the keys to the double-wide metal entry doors in his pocket, ready to hand over to Chessie.

He'd really pushed his men today, eager to get the place locked up after that circular saw had grown legs and walked off the site, not because he hated losing equipment, although he did, but because it reminded him that Chessie lived alone in the apartment over the shop.

The woman didn't even have an alarm system. Whether she was trusting or naive wasn't the question. The question was how could he convince both Chessie and Marylou that the alarm system he'd just ordered installed throughout the building was worth the money it would add to the final bill. People who didn't have alarm systems usually believed they didn't need alarm systems, or they were too unreliable, or they didn't want to have to bother with codes and setting and disarming the systems.

Well, tough. Chessie was not going to spend more than another two days without an alarm system. She'd just have to get used to working with the keypad, that's all. She was an intelligent woman. She could do that. Because he needed her to be safe.

Jace blinked at that last thought. He was getting a little too involved here, wasn't he? This was just another job. Chessie was just... He didn't know what she was. He'd get her out of his head if he could. The problem was he'd yet to find a way to do that.

"What's up, Jace? You're looking at the job like it's the enemy. We're ahead of schedule thanks to the dry weather, and now it can rain whenever it wants to, and we're still good. Well, except for the siding and the roof shingles and the rain gutters, but you know what I mean."

Jace snapped back to the moment. "Yeah, Carl, I know. And nothing's up. That's probably what worries me. There's always at least one problem, but we haven't hit it yet. You're all ready to head out? I'll see you tomorrow." He turned to give a wave to the rest of the crew. "Thanks for a great day, guys."

When they were gone, Jace unlocked the doors and took one more look around the interior of what was to be a twenty-by-twenty-four-foot square glorified storeroom. About the size of an average two-car garage. Four walls, three windows, one double-width door wide enough for deliveries. Above it, the workroom, where Marylou and Chessie would do whatever it is people do with bits of lace and glue guns.

Jace looked at the ceiling. Looked at the door leading into the existing stockroom or whatever it was called; the place with the rows of gowns lined up inside clear plastic bags, the shelves stacked with boxes.

"From the back door, through this room, through the stockroom, down the hall, up the stairs, through the apartment, into the new workroom—and then through the apartment, down the stairs, back along the hall, through the stockroom, into the storage room. And, going either up or down, probably with both arms full of boxes and bags. That's nuts!"

The client tells you what they want, and you give the client what he or she wants. But, damn, if they hadn't seen this, he should have. Maybe it was all those gowns and veils and wedding stuff, spooking him so that he'd just wanted to take his necessary measurements and get the hell out of there.

Once more looking up at the ceiling, Jace mentally sketched out the plan of the upper room, how the enlarged bathroom was configured, the new doorway from bathroom to workroom, the small hallway he'd considered in order to provide more shelving space. Was there room for a set of stairs? He'd make room.

And he'd eat the expense on this one, because he should have seen it. He should have seen a lot of things he hadn't seen because of those damn gowns he had to fight his way through every time he walked inside the place.

Not the gowns. He had to stop trying to say that he was this man's man, rough and tumble, the sort of guy who just naturally developed a twitch when forced to be around delicate and white and frilly.

He got twitchy around marriage, that's where he got nervous. It even smelled like a wedding inside the building. All flowery and fragile and feminine. Every time he went inside he felt like the proverbial bull in a china shop.

Or like a onetime loser in no hurry to make a second mistake.

Maybe he should stay away. Get the job done and move on. Stop looking at Chessie Burton as some sort of challenge, maybe a test he had to pass, or something, to prove that sex was sex and there didn't need to be any consideration other than mutual pleasure.

She turned him on. He turned her on. That's the way it was for men and women. Sometimes. An instant sexual connection. There was no rhyme or reason for why that happened. It just did.

The trick was not to talk to her too much. Not to get to know her. Last night had been a mistake. A big one. The minute he'd loaded the tools into the basement he should have taken off, gone home, opened a cold one and then another and maybe another, until he stopped thinking about Tennis Anyone being alone upstairs with Chessie in her apartment, planning his next serve, his next volley, all while hoping to get to the final set and the winner's trophy.

And then, probably because she'd already had one move made on her that night, and one was probably more than enough, he'd decided to be the good guy. He hadn't decided that immediately; he'd certainly had other ideas. But she'd had that fragile look about her again, the same one he'd seen when he'd walked in on her and Marylou and Marylou had been talking about some guy named Rick.

He didn't know who Rick was. He just knew he didn't like him.

So he'd stuck around, thinking he could be the handy shoulder she could lean on, and he'd ended up sharing milk and cookies and conversation that had somehow lasted until close to two o'clock in the morning.

Without him ever once looking at the clock above the stove and thinking he had better things to do.

He'd kissed her good-night after she'd walked him to the side door, and he handed her the keys…and that had been it. That and the drive home and the second-guessing he'd gone through until exhaustion finally put an end to it.

Chessie Burton kissed like a woman who knew what she wanted.

But those big blue eyes told another story.

She was vulnerable. Yes, that was it. Vulnerable. Jace didn't know why she was, but he was sure he was right. The question was, what was he going to do about it?

Walking away was one option, but it didn't much appeal to him. Taking advantage of that vulnerability would brand him the worst sort of loser. Which left one other option. He could be her friend.

Damn. Couldn't there be a fourth option there some-where?

"Hi. You're still here? Wow, look at this. Doors and windows and everything."

Jace shook his head slightly, trying to rid his brain of thoughts that didn't make him much of a hero. "Hi, Chessie," he said, slowly turning to face her. "I was just checking out a few things before bringing you the keys." He held them out to her. "There you go. Keys."

She took them, slid them into the pocket of her skirt, the one that ended just above her knees, and left the rest of those long, incredibly straight legs bare to the tips of her painted toes.

"You shouldn't be barefoot out here," he told her, re-adjusting his gaze to her face, but taking the leisurely way all the way up her body. "You could step on something sharp."

She lifted the shoes she was holding. "I know, but I didn't want to risk my heels trying to climb in here. Is there going to be a step down from the doors to the driveway?"

"No, we still need to fill in around the foundation. Then it'll be a straight shot into here. You wouldn't want to have to navigate steps when you're loaded down with… whatever you'll be loaded down with. Speaking of which, you should have a staircase to the second floor in here. It would make your life a lot easier."

Chessie frowned as she looked up at the ceiling—just as he had done. "You know, you're right. Is it too late?"

Too late, too soon. Too fast, too slow. To stay or to go, that's the question. It wasn't Shakespeare, but it was honest.

"Why don't you sleep on it," Jace heard himself say.

"That's probably a good idea," she agreed, bracing one hand against him as she slipped her shoes back on. "Thanks."

The two of them headed for the open doors. "Here, let me help," he said, and then scooped her up and carried her so that she didn't have to try to navigate the two-foot drop down to the jumble of dirt and stones and probably nails and staples that were mixed in with the rest of the debris.

She put her arms around his neck, not fighting him, and laughed. "Leave it to me," she said, "to be carried over the threshold on the way *out* instead of in. Thank you again, kind sir."

He carried her until he reached the cement pathway leading to the side door of the salon and then reluctantly put her down. *Very* reluctantly.

He kept his hands at her waist.

She didn't remove her hands from his shoulders.

Their combined posture wasn't awkward. But it was tense. And intense.

"I probably should tell you," he said, taking option number four, the one that had just occurred to him: honesty. "I'm not looking for a long-term relationship."

"So I'm up one on you. I'm not looking for any kind of relationship," Chessie replied, her huge blue eyes looking so open and honest he knew he had to believe her. "I don't know what happened—almost happened—yesterday in my bedroom. I really don't. And I don't think I want to dissect it, either."

"Last night was easier," Jace said, rubbing his hands up and down her long, slim back, then settling against her waist once more, his fingertips aware of the small central dip near the base of her spine. If he just moved his hands a little lower...

"It was nice," Chessie agreed, her voice sounding a bit breathless. "Talking."

"And dipping," he added, smiling. "Those were great cookies."

"I'll tell Berthe, and she'll make some just for you. But I still have half a tin upstairs."

"I am still hungry, Chess. But not for cookies."

And with that admission, tense and intense began the slide toward inevitable....

"Yes...I know." She was sort of kneading at his shoulders now. "It's not as if we planned..."

"Hell, no," he said, maybe taking honesty too far. "I mean, that is—I don't know what I mean. I was half joking yesterday. Being stupid. I never thought stealing one kiss would lead to—"

"Almost lead to. We're not there yet," she corrected, still with her hands on his shoulders. "It's all right, I understand. We don't have to do anything else about it if you don't want to."

"Are you trying to let me down easy, or save yourself?" *Now where the hell had that come from?*

Her mouth dropped open. "I wasn't trying to do anything, Jace Edwards. You started this. Yesterday, and again just now. Of the two days, I have to say I liked yesterday a lot better. Does that answer your stupid question?"

He had to swallow before he could speak again, hope his dry mouth would even open, yet alone be able to form words. Not giving a damn if someone might be watching, he stepped closer, pushed up against her. "You want this? To happen, I mean. No strings, no…no nothing? Just to happen? Just tonight. One crazy, stupid night, and then we can get it out of our systems, move on with our lives."

She just looked at him, her eyes nearly black, her pupils had gone so wide. Didn't say a word. Didn't move, didn't draw away. But her breathing suddenly became shallow, almost labored.

"I want it to happen," he said at last. "I don't know what it is, I don't know why I can't get you out of my head. But I can't. I need to see you naked. I need to touch you…everywhere. Not want, Chess. *Need*. All I can think about is the way we'd be together. I know it would be good. We'd be so good."

At last she closed her eyes. But then she opened them once more, those huge blue windows to her soul. What did he see there? What would he see there when he was deep inside her, taking them both to the conclusion that was so obvious he could nearly see it all inside his head now?

He watched as a tantalizing hint of color appeared on her bare upper chest, a flush of desire that fueled his own.

"I can almost feel you inside me now," she said, her voice low, husky. "It's sex, Jace. I've heard that it happens this way sometimes. It's just never happened to me. I want it to happen to me. I want to be wild, and free, and maybe even dangerous. Like you said. One night. I wouldn't ask anything else. I don't want anything else. I just want to… let go. Let go of everything inside me, every inhibition, any fears, any thought of shame or right or wrong. I've never thought I could, or even wanted to. But now I just need to let it all go. One night."

"One night only," he agreed, even as something inside him revolted at the thought. He pushed the reluctance behind a door in his mind and shut it. She was right, she had to be right. It was sex, that's all. There was nothing more there, nothing else between them. "When? Don't say tomorrow, Chess. I don't want to give you time to change your mind."

"Or you. We close at seven. You could stop by around nine."

"For dinner?" he asked, watching the corners of her mouth turning up into a smile that should be illegal, it was that blatantly provocative. Just looking into those eyes, seeing that small smile, had him so hard he was nearly in pain.

Finally, she stepped away from him, almost dancing as she turned toward the shop. "Find your own dinner, Jace Edwards. I thought we were discussing dessert. I'll leave the side door open, so just come on up."

Chapter Five

What did one wear to a planned and mutual seduction?

Clearly nothing Chessie had thus far tried on and discarded as being too dull, too plain, too boring…or too hard to get out of, which definitely was something to be considered when dressing to be undressed. You never saw a seduction scene in a movie where the seductee was wearing a turtleneck sweater, for crying out loud…

She lowered her head into her hands and wondered when it was that she'd lost what was left of her mind. She'd probably gathered it up by mistake when she'd been busily tossing all of her common sense into some mental trash bin.

She'd never been promiscuous. She wasn't sure she even knew anyone who had ever been promiscuous.

Well, okay, there was Marylou. Except that wasn't true, either. Marylou had married the men she'd slept with. At least three of them, anyway.

"Stay on point, stay focused, get dressed," Chessie told herself, looking around her bedroom and most of her wardrobe, which was scattered all over the place. She went into cleanup mode, still dressed in her bathrobe, still with nothing to wear.

"I'm hopeless," she said at last, plopping down on her now cleaned-off bed and lying back to stare at the ceiling. Were those dead bugs in the glass light shade of the hideously old and out-of-date overhead light? Well, of course they were. There were always a couple of kamikaze bugs that managed to work their way through the window screens and dive bomb the lightbulbs.

Was this the sort of thing femme fatales thought about when they knew there soon would be a man in their bedroom? Probably not.

But since she wasn't a femme fatale, Chessie got up, stood on the mattress and unscrewed the light shade.

The light shade slipped from her hands, fell onto the mattress, where it bounced and turned over, and a half-dozen bugs—toes up and deader than doornails—scattered all over her freshly changed sheets.

Chessie wanted to cry.

She wasn't cut out for this, none of it. She didn't have what it took to arrange a night of mad monkey sex with a stranger and then pull it off as if it was nothing out of the ordinary.

She wasn't that kind of girl.

"No," she told herself as she stripped the top sheet and headed for the linen closet. "You're the kind of girl who *wishes* you could be that kind of girl. Just once. One time. A fling. A…a moment in time. Every girl should have one, shouldn't she?"

Knowing the answer to that would depend on who she asked, Chessie erased the question from her mind, remade the bed and headed back to her closet.

"You want him," she said softly, giving in at last to the inevitable. "It isn't right, it isn't wrong. It just *is*. You looked at him and you wanted him. Bang. Instant. Pure unbridled lust. He turned you on. You turned him on. You're a good girl who wants to be a bad girl just this one time. One itty-bitty time, and then you can go back to dull and boring. And you're damn well not going to back down now, so just knock it off, Burton, dig into this closet and find yourself some sleaze."

The second-floor windows were dark, but as he walked up the cement pathway to the side door he thought he could make out some sort of flickering light behind the glass, as if she'd set out candles everywhere. Setting the scene, he decided, and then decided that was all right with him.

There'd be time for lights later, once she'd lost any lingering inhibitions. Then he'd look his fill, touch her in all her most intimate places, watch her response. Hear her soft moans. Drink from her as he spread her, teased her, as she raised her hips to him...

He'd never thought like this. Had never felt like this. Sex. For the sake of sex. For the glory of it, the white-hot heat of it, the insatiable need of it.

He'd pick her up, lie on his back on her bed and watch as she slowly settled herself over him, as she slipped her own hands between them and pleasured herself even as she pleasured him...

He'd married the first woman he'd ever slept with, because that was the right thing to do. He'd had encounters since the divorce. But they'd been forgettable; just necessary release, and they hadn't been all that frequent. He hadn't been a monk, but he'd poured all his energies, all his desire, into his business, and that hadn't left much time for anything else. Or anyone else.

On her bed...in her shower...on the kitchen table where they'd shared cookies and milk and conversation. He'd dribble milk between her breasts, watch it flow slowly down, into her navel, and then he'd lick it off....

It was sex. That's what he wanted. That's what she wanted. Two people. Two busy people with businesses to build, futures to work toward. Definite plans.

Two lonely people who'd been on the outside of life for so long....

He climbed the stairs and knocked on the door to her apartment, the bouquet of summer flowers feeling inadequate, maybe a stupid gesture. Then again, a package of condoms wasn't exactly a great hostess gift.

He was smiling at his own ridiculous thought as the door opened.

She smiled back at him, and then turned to walk a few steps back into the candlelit living room.

She was wearing a halter top that tied behind her neck and at her waist. A pair of shorts whose length probably inspired the name. Her feet were bare. Her coppery hair still damp and curling around her head.

She was fresh from her shower, and he could smell the mix of soap and some light scent that reminded him of summer nights at his parents' lake cottage.

Her back still to him, she ran her hands down the sides of her body, down to her thighs and then back up again, skimming over her buttocks before they disappeared in front of her and her shoulders hunched slightly.

He knew what she was doing; she was cupping her own breasts in her hands.

She half turned, smiling at him over her shoulder.

He briefly wondered where she'd locked up her inhibitions, and then just hoped she'd lost the key.

"More," he said tightly. "Turn all the way around. Look at me."

She did as he asked, her hands still cupping herself. Her thumbs moving as she gently squeezed her breasts together.

Jace knew he'd been put on notice.

He dropped the bouquet somewhere in the general

vicinity of a table he was pretty sure was beside the door, and then kicked that door shut.

He was already unbuttoning his shirt as he walked to where she was standing in the middle of the room.

She reached behind her and undid the top closing of her halter top, letting it fall to her waist.

The candlelight flickered warmly against her bare skin. She wore no bra.

His shirt hit the floor and she stepped forward, placing both her palms against his rib cage.

His muscles flinched involuntarily beneath her touch, and she smiled. It was a secret smile; he couldn't read her thoughts.

He reached behind her and undid the second tie, and then went to work on the row of buttons that made up the front closure of her shorts. She wore no underwear.

Even as she undid his belt, she had nearly rid him of his slacks before he could grab one of the foil packets from his pocket. If she had waited another moment, until she'd closed her hand over him, he wouldn't have remembered safety precautions at all.

They had all night. They hadn't discussed any time limit, but he was sure they both knew it. And they'd use every minute of that night.

But now wasn't all night. Now was the moment they'd both ached for. Now was the explosion that couldn't wait. She'd signaled as much to him, and he hadn't missed the sign.

He picked her up and she straddled his waist even as

she clamped her arms close around his neck. He backed up toward the door, turning at the last moment and putting her against it, holding her there as he fumbled with the damn protection, his hands shaking as desire nearly overcame him.

Finally...finally...

"Aahhh, yes..."

Her hold on him tightened as he moved inside her. She bit at his neck as he pressed her against the door, driving into her without mercy, and she took everything he had and still wordlessly begged for more, her fingernails digging into his skin, her low moans spurring him on and on and on.

And then, suddenly, her entire body seemed to go quiet, and she simply clung to him, not breathing but just holding on, as if something momentous was about to occur, something she had been seeking getting close, closer, and if she moved, if she breathed, it might not come.

He wouldn't let that happen.

He slipped his hands down to cup her buttocks, careful to hold her in place as he gave her all he had to give; deeper, faster, harder, until she cried out in near triumph as she found what she'd been seeking.... "Yes, yes, *yes*."

He felt his own climax then, an explosion and a release that nearly buckled his knees as, together, they sank to the floor, still locked together.

There was nothing but the sounds of two people

attempting to catch their breath, and then no sound at all.

Until he heard her giggle.

Jace rolled onto his back, pulling her along with him, and saw her smiling face looking down into his. "What?" he asked her, cupping her buttocks and pressing her against him.

"Nothing," she said, and then giggled again. "Okay, something. I feel…I feel like something out of a bad movie. Did we really just do that?"

"Some of my memories are a little hazy, but I think I'll always remember all of this one. Yes, we really just did do that."

She laid her cheek against his chest. "Amazing."

"Why, thank you, ma'am," he said, and planted a kiss on the top of her head. Their first kiss of the night, actually, which was pretty amazing all by itself. He had some catching up to do.

"Not you. Us. It. If you hadn't taken your shirt off by yourself, I probably would have ripped it off. With my teeth. I—I just jumped you, with no provocation. I should be so ashamed."

Jace thought about this for a moment. "Don't forget the foreplay."

She lifted her head once more, her curls falling into her eyes. "I don't remember any foreplay."

"Sure you do. Tell me you haven't been thinking about what would happen here every second of every minute since we had that little discussion outside earlier. Foreplay."

"You mean while I was mixing up the mother of the bride with the mother of the groom, and then put the wrong gown on the bride?"

"I went through a red light," Jace admitted. "You're lucky I'm here at all, and not lying in a ditch somewhere."

Chessie began nibbling at the side of his chin. "Thank heaven for small favors. Do you want to get up now?"

She wiggled herself against him as she pushed up on her hands.

"Not if you keep that up, no," he told her, but then he managed to reach down and grab her behind the knees, lifting her as he got to his feet. "I'd ask you to point me toward the bedroom, but I already know where it is."

She snuggled in close. "I guess I should have asked this question earlier. Are you insatiable?"

"I didn't think so until yesterday. Maybe."

She laughed again, that free, easy laugh he'd never heard before, the one that did something more to his heart than it did to his libido. "Oh, that's good…."

Chessie awoke hungry, but not for food. Food was unnecessary to life at the moment. But something else was.

She lifted her head from the pillow—how did the pillow get to the bottom of the bed? How did she end up at the bottom of the bed? Oh. Right. She remembered now.

Jace had turned her around, and then slowly pulled her up the length of his torso, belly to belly, as he laid back against the brass headboard, spreading her legs as he did so, and then sliding her legs up and over his shoulders as he…and then she…

That had been interesting. But, then, he'd been running out of condoms. Good thing she had bought some herself. Even better that she hadn't told him immediately, or else things might not have gotten so…interesting.

The green digital glow of the bedside clock told her it was a little after three in the morning. A sweep of her bare legs across the mattress told her that she was alone in the bed. The immediate sense of loss was eased when she at last realized what had awakened her.

Jace was in the shower.

Alone.

Poor boy.

Chessie had inhibitions. Everyone did. She was by nature modest, shy about her body and not very adventuresome.

But Chessie wasn't here, thank God. Chessie the good girl, the "I would never do *that!*" girl was on a long trip somewhere, and the just-born Wishful Chessie, the Wild Chessie, the "Oh, why the hell not!" Chessie was in residence for the night.

And she was going to make every minute of that night count!

She might have wrapped herself in the top sheet, if she could have found it, but since she was pretty sure one end of it was still tied to the bedpost, she just rolled off the mattress and headed for the bathroom.

Her breath caught as she saw Jace standing in the clear-glass shower stall that hid little from her view, his back turned to her. She'd had his body, every inch of it, touched and tasted and savored, but there was something about seeing him when he thought himself unobserved that hit her like a punch to the stomach.

And lower.

His muscles weren't immense, overdeveloped. He didn't look like a weight lifter. He was simply fit and healthy, a hard worker whose body reflected that.

She thought his sun-avoiding tush looked pretty cute, though, where the rest of him was so beautifully, evenly tanned.

Chessie looked down at her own body, wondering if maybe she wasn't pushing things, daring to be naked with him in the light of the bathroom. His perfection up against her ho-hum body. Not that he'd seemed disappointed that she wasn't especially...lush.

He poured some shampoo into his hand and raised both hands to his head, rubbing in the shampoo as he turned slightly in the shower. She could see his chest now, watch his muscles move as he worked in the shampoo, as streams of bubbles began running down his neck, over his chest, skimming that damned six-pack that had gotten her into all of this in the first place.

"Okay, that does it, I'm ready," she said out loud, heading for the shower stall.

She stepped inside, lifting the soft net ball from its resting place, and quickly loaded it with liquid soap as he watched her, his hands still on his head, his smile of welcome curling her toes.

"Okay, whose fantasy is this—yours or mine?" he asked her, blinking soap out of his eyes. He even blinked sexily.

"I don't have fantasies," she told him, knowing that was a fib. She hadn't had fantasies until she'd met him. Now all she did was fantasize; she should be washing out her mind with the scrubbie. When you got right down to it, the man was a menace. "What's yours?"

"Nope. If you won't share, neither will I. A man has his pride."

"Yeah, right. And you say that with shampoo all over your head. But never fear, I think I have some idea. Stop me if I'm wrong…"

Dropping to her knees, she proceeded to wash him, paying very careful attention to…detail. Until he did actually stop her by taking the net ball from her and returning the favor as she hung on to his shoulders, because otherwise her rubbery knees would have betrayed her and she would have slipped to the floor. He slid the net over her chest, rubbed it in circles around her straining nipples…insinuated it between her legs and gently stroked, stroked, stroked. Until she whimpered and let go. Let it all just…go.

Jace woke at six and crept out of the bedroom, heading downstairs for the duffel bag he'd brought with him, the one with his work clothes in it. He hadn't taken it upstairs because that would make it seem as if he'd planned to stay the night. Which he hadn't planned. He'd just hoped.

He was pouring his first cup of coffee when Chessie appeared in the kitchen doorway, sleep rumpled and wearing a T-shirt three sizes too big for her. On the front were the words Keep Back. I Don't Just Hate Mornings. I Kill Morning People.

She pointed to his cup and he handed it over to her, then watched her slide onto the same chair she'd sat on the night they'd shared milk and cookies. She held the mug in both hands and sipped from it, blew on the surface of the coffee, doggedly sipped again.

He poured himself another cup and sat down across from her. "So. When is it safe to talk to you?"

Still with her hands on the mug, she straightened her index finger.

"One more sip? One more minute? One more hour? I should come back next month?"

She finally put down the cup, closing her eyes and letting out a long sigh. "I feel like I've been shipwrecked, and then the waves tossed me around on the rocks for a couple of hours before spitting me out on the beach."

He tried not to smile. "This is why we also work, eat and sleep. Constant sex, great as it is, could kill us in a couple of days."

She nodded her agreement. "You look good, though. I checked myself in the bathroom mirror before I came out here. I look like something you might find stuck to the bottom of one of those work boots of yours. That's not fair."

"I think you look beautiful. You are beautiful. Everywhere," Jace said before he could edit his thoughts.

Suddenly, inexplicably, she looked shy. Her eyelids lowering, her head turning a little away from him, that damnably adorable blush creeping into her cheeks.

"I'm not allowed to say that I think you're beautiful? Maybe we should have gone over the rules a little more."

She bit her lips together, shook her head. "No, it's all right. Thank you."

"You're welcome," Jace said, his voice sounding a little hard, even to himself. But he could take a hint. She wanted him gone. He got to his feet. "So…?"

"So…" Chessie repeated, putting down her own cup and getting to her feet. "I guess that's—" her hands fluttered as she seemed to hunt for the right words "—I guess that's…it?"

"Yeah." Jace wanted to kick something. Starting with his own backside. "I guess that's it. We were right. It was good. We were good."

Chessie reached for her coffee cup and held it up in front of her, like some sort of shield. "I think so. Yes."

He couldn't tell what she was thinking. And she wasn't helping him, damn it.

"And now you're having second thoughts and you just wish I'd get the hell out of here, right?"

She blinked rapidly, obviously trying to hold back tears. And then she nodded.

"Fine. That was the agreement. We both agreed. I blew out your damn candles for you, but the flowers are dead. Now I'll get out of your way."

Jace slammed out of the apartment, taking out some of his anger and frustration by slamming her front door and then the side door leading outside. Neither slam helped.

What the hell was the matter with him? He'd just had the kind of night most men dream of, for crying out loud. And with no strings attached, no promises, no recriminations, no worries about letting the woman down easy.

And he'd gone into the thing with both eyes open, had even laid down conditions of his own.

She'd gotten out of her system whatever she'd needed out of her system, and he'd had the best sex of his life, the most willing partner, his every fantasy played out and more. He should be whistling, eager to tell his buddies about his great night. His big score.

He turned and looked up at the blank windows.

That was it. Done. Over. He couldn't say she hadn't been true to her word.

She hadn't even suggested they kiss each other goodbye....

Chessie walked around the apartment with a plastic clothes basket, dumping burned-down candles into it as she went. They mashed down the sad, wilted flowers she hadn't even noticed last night, hadn't thanked him for and couldn't possibly revive.

Every once in a while she lifted the hem of her sleep shirt and wiped at her tear-wet cheeks. Once, just once, she'd used it to blow her nose.

Why was she crying? She'd gotten what she'd wanted, hadn't she?

And Jace had more than lived up to expectations. He'd been in turn forceful, leisurely, attentive, demanding. He'd been playful and even a little tender. He'd satisfied her every need, even needs she hadn't known she had.

He'd made her feel playful, sensual, exciting, wantonly, sinfully sexy and, yes, beautiful. Desirable. He'd made her purr, and moan and cry out in ecstasy so overpowering she thought she might die of it.

He'd kissed her. Oh, how he'd kissed her. She could taste his hunger.

She'd given as good as she got, or at least she hoped so. He'd seemed to think so.

Two relative strangers, sharing intimacies that brought a fiery blush to not just her cheeks but to her entire body now, as she relived that first, frantic coupling, the silliness in the kitchen that had turned grittily serious and intense. The way she had only half jokingly loosely looped his wrists together and then tied the sheet to the headboard, and then told him just what she wanted to do with him… and he'd laughingly let her.

She could still taste him. Smell him. Feel the heat of him.

She wished she'd never done it, any of it. It had been wonderful. It had been body over mind.

Now the pleasure was a memory, and she felt strangely bereft, empty. Even as she'd been insatiable all of the night, feeling everything she had always wanted to feel... there had been something, some elusive something, always remaining just beyond her reach. Incomplete.

For everything they'd done, everything they'd shared, she felt somehow cheated. Did he feel the same way? Was that why he'd looked at her so strangely just before he left, as if he was angry with her?

She'd never know.

Because she'd never be able to look at him again.

Chessie bent down to pick up the crinoline that had slipped out of her hand as she'd attempted to suspend it from the clips on the hanger.

She moved like a woman twice her age, maybe three times her age. Every muscle in her body ached, nearly screamed out to her to for God's sake sit down on something soft and leave us alone for a while. And it would have to be something soft, because she was still swollen between her legs, and almost exquisitely tender.

"How do rabbits stand it?" she muttered under her breath.

Her arms felt leaden, she kept getting small, painful cramps in her right hand she didn't want to imagine the source of, and her bottom lip was sort of tingly. It would be nice if she could get some blood to flow to her head, because it all seemed to be settled lower, half in anticipation, half because it was probably too tired to pump that high.

"Are you planning to spend the rest of the day down there?"

Chessie closed her eyes. Wasn't this Marylou's day off? Hadn't Ted come home from Vegas yet? Hadn't they celebrated his homecoming in bed? Marylou was nearly twice Chessie's age, and yet she seemed fresh, her usual bouncy self. Maybe she took special vitamins. She'd have to ask her for the brand name.

"I was looking for stray straight pins. You know how they can hide in the carpet in here," Chessie lied, and then willed herself to her feet, biting back a groan. "Why are you here?"

"Jace called me. He wants to discuss adding a staircase or something. And a security system."

"Well, good-good-goody for Jace." Good old Jace. Mr. Professional, already back on the job, and with no ill effects. No jet lag for Jace Edwards. No self-recrimination or second thoughts, either, Chessie decided.

Men were just wired differently, that's all. Where did she think the saying "Wham, bam, thank you, ma'am" had come from, if it wasn't so typical of men to take what they could get and then walk away without a qualm? Women didn't have that luxury. Women always got stuck with feelings of guilt.

And maybe some regret, sadness and a wish that things could have worked out differently…even if they didn't plan on or even want things to work out differently. Maybe if, on top of all the great sex, they didn't actually *like* the guy, damn it.

"Goody-goody for Jace? You sound like you're thinking of roasting the man on a spit. What's the problem? You don't like him?"

Chessie took refuge in partial fib, partial truth. "I don't even think about him. I just don't want a security system. They don't work. We've got great locks. But if someone wants to get in here, they'll get in here. And at least I won't be setting off the alarm by mistake when I open a window or decide to get a glass of water in the middle of the night. And what happens if I buy a cat?"

"You're thinking about buying a cat? How many cats? Old maids surround themselves with cats."

"I'm not buying a cat. I was just saying, giving a for-instance."

"Good. But as for the security system, Jace already ordered it, probably knowing I'd agree with him, which I do. The wiring goes in tomorrow."

"Damn." Chessie didn't want a security system, didn't want to give up without a fight, but to fight it she'd have to see Jace, talk to Jace. And that wasn't happening! "All right, all right, you just do what you want. But you'll have to meet with him by yourself. I'm really too busy."

Then she tried to stifle a yawn, but it got away from her.

Marylou looked at her, tilting her head to one side as

if examining her for flaws. "You had sex last night, didn't you?"

Pushing a hand against the small of her back, Chessie stretched, or at least tried to stretch. "What gave me away? The soft glow in my eyes, my secret smile?"

"There are bags under your eyes and you're not smiling, probably because your bottom lip is puffy and there's what looks like some badly camouflaged beard-stubble rash on your chin. What were you trying to do, make up for a year of abstinence in one night?"

It had been two years since she'd been with a man, but Chessie wasn't about to share that piece of information. Her friends pitied her enough as it was. They'd all thought the same thing—Chessie would be much better, happier, if she only had a man in her life.

Was that sexist? Antifeminist? Or just *honest?* Besides, as far as Marylou had seemed to be concerned, it wasn't a man in her life that Chessie needed, it was just a man.

And until this morning, when Jace had looked at her with that odd, unreadable expression in his eyes, and then had slammed out of her apartment, Chessie had pretty much agreed with Marylou's assertion.

Except now it was even worse than it had been before Jace. Now she felt twice as empty inside. Not because she wouldn't have sex with Jace again. Because she wouldn't be able to talk with him again in that same easy way, smile with him, look forward to seeing him. Sex was great, no doubts there. But companionship, caring, sharing—in the long run they were all better.

"I can't win with you, can I, Marylou?" Chessie asked as she walked across the hall and into her office, taking refuge by sitting down—gingerly—behind her desk. "First I'm not getting enough, as you have at least once so delicately called it, and now I'm getting too much."

Marylou sat down on the chair on the far side of the desk, crossing her long legs at the knee, her right foot moving in a slow kick, her backless heeled sandal dangling. "Moderation in all things, Chess. Living hard and dying young is about as bad as living forever and never really being alive. One's too short, the other's too long. You want to concentrate on the just right."

"Now I feel like you're handing me the X-rated version of *Goldilocks and the Three Bears*."

Marylou kept her expression solemn. "We could learn a lot from fairy tales, you know. Especially about wolves. Wolves in sheeps' clothing, wolves that huff and puff and are really mostly filled with hot air. Wolves that pretend they're something they're not. *The Boy Who Cried Wolf.* I could go on. Please, stop me."

"Happily. In fact, let's just drop the subject completely, okay?"

"Really? I'd thought you'd want to tell me just a little about Toby. I'm not asking for the juicy details—although I wouldn't mind, if you feel like sharing. But you two have obviously hit it off, at least in one area. So, when am I going to meet him? Ted and I thought maybe a nice dinner party next week? Elizabeth and Will, Claire and Nick, Ted and me, you and Toby. Elizabeth is going to be having that baby in a few months, and Lord only knows when we'd be able to do it again."

Chessie's early-warning system started clanging. Marylou was pushing her into a corner, pushing her to produce Toby, knowing damn well that Toby hadn't been the one she'd been with last night. Chessie knew it; Marylou knew it. How did Marylou know? What had given her away? Why did she have to hang around with such smart friends?

Still, Chessie tried to hedge, play for time. "Don't try to put this one on Elizabeth. You just want to check him out."

Marylou shrugged in her elegant way. "And that's so wrong? We're friends, Chess, but I'm old enough to be your mother—not that anyone else has to know that, and start counting on their fingers. You're on the rebound, and I don't want to see you rush into anything."

"Rebound?" Chessie laughed. "On the rebound from what? Who, I mean."

"Rick Peters, of course. Now that he's back in town."

Chessie sat back in her chair, stunned. Marylou wasn't giving up on this one, was she? "Rick dumped me six years ago, Marylou. That would have to be a record-long rebound."

"Okay, then look me in the eye and tell me you were with this Toby guy last night."

Chessie lowered her gaze to the desktop.

"Uh-huh. I knew it. I can be wrong once in a while,

but not that often. Now tell me who it really was, not that I don't already know, unfortunately. It was Rick, wasn't it?"

Chessie tried to blink back her tears, but one escaped onto her cheek, and she rubbed at it angrily. "Marylou, don't. It doesn't matter who it was. It's what I did. It was a mistake, a stupid, impulsive, crazy mistake, I feel horribly embarrassed, and I really, really don't want to talk about it."

Her friend got up and quickly came around the desk to wrap Chessie in a fierce hug. "Shh, it's all right, sweetheart. Water under the bridge, that's all he was, right, and it's over now, he's finally out of your system. Everyone makes mistakes, but they're not the end of the world. Nobody knows but us two, and we won't talk about it. Not ever again. It's over. Now why don't you go upstairs and take a nap. I can hold down the fort here."

Sniffling, nodding, Chessie disentangled herself from Marylou's embrace and headed for the stairs. She got as far as the bedroom, as far as the rumpled bed, before she began to cry in earnest.

Chapter Six

Jace had very nearly taken his thumb off because he hadn't been paying attention as he trimmed a two-by-four on the circular saw, and had just figuratively taken George's head off for asking a simple question.

"You all right, Jace?" Carl asked from behind him as Jace watched George disappear back inside the addition. "He just wanted to know if you wanted to knock through the wall into Ms. Burton's bedroom today."

Jace turned to look at his friend, feeling sheepish, stupid. A total jerk. "I know. I need to go apologize to him."

"I'll handle it. You've got a lot on your mind."

"It's that obvious, huh?" Jace asked, rubbing at the side of his neck. "Carl, how long have you been married?"

The older man's eyebrows rose, nearly disappearing beneath his hard hat. "Married? Who's— That is, I don't know. I should, but I always first have to think how old Carl Jr. is, and then add a year, even though it was really only seven months, not that my Mildred wouldn't kill me for saying that. Okay, forty. We're married for forty years this coming September."

"Then you have experience. With women, I mean."

"I do?" Carl tipped back his hard hat, grinning widely. "Coulda fooled me. Coulda fooled Millie, too, because she's always telling me I don't have a clue. You buy one blender for an anniversary present twenty years ago, and you never live it down. What's the problem?"

Jace opened the cooler and pulled out two bottles of water, handed one to Carl. "I'm not sure," he said as they took up seats on top of the picnic table, under the shade of the trees, propping their work boots on the bench. "I don't think they are, either. About what they want, I mean."

Carl twisted off the bottle top and took a long drink before pressing the chilled plastic against his forehead. "Oh. That. I mean, good luck with that. Millie will tell me I should know what's bothering her and won't tell me because I should know, but I'm pretty sure she doesn't tell me because she doesn't know, either. Until she finally figures it out. Usually by figuring out that it was all my fault, whatever it was. Then, of course, she tells me it's too late for me to apologize."

Jace slanted a look at his employee and friend. "You're kidding, right?"

Carl raised his hard hat. "See this head? It would be full of gray hair if she hadn't driven me bald. So, no, I'm not kidding."

Jace watched Carl replace his hard hat. "But you love her?"

Carl looked at him sharply, his dark brown eyes flashing. "Damn straight. I'd be lost without her, that's my Millie. I just gave up trying to understand her. So what's going on, Jace? You got women problems?"

"In theory? No. In theory, Carl, I should be one of the happiest men on the planet."

"I'm looking at your face here, pal, and I gotta tell you something. If that's happy, as my granddaddy used to say, I'll take vanilla. I didn't know you were seeing anyone."

"I'm not," Jace said, rubbing the water bottle between his palms. "Not seriously, anyway. You know, no long-term commitment. And not anymore." *Probably the shortest-term commitment in history,* Jace thought, grimacing. "We'd agreed on that from the start. Only I think maybe she might be changing her mind."

"Uh-oh." Carl waggled his fingers close to Jace's face. "Just when you think you're out, they drag you— What's the rest of that?"

Jace pushed his hands away. "Cut that out, you nut, I'm trying to be serious here."

"Serious as a funeral. Yeah, we noticed. So you're trying to figure out how to dump her, let her down easy?"

Jace looked at Carl for a long moment, and then shook

his head. "Millie has my complete sympathy. Tell her that for me, will you? No, I'm not trying to let her down easy. She's gone, it's over. Except I don't think she wants it to be over."

"But you do. Help me out here, bro. Am I getting any of this right?"

Jace unfolded his lean body and got to his feet. "No, but that's all right. Neither am I. Okay, back to work. Damn. Here comes Marylou. Why don't you guys break for lunch. On me. Just bring me something back. Not much, I'm really not hungry. And tell George I'm sorry, okay? I'll catch him later, but you tell him now, so he doesn't worry."

"The man is a worrier. Hi, Marylou, good seeing you again," Carl said, and then took off, pocketing the twenties Jace had handed him.

Jace quickly put on his shirt.

"Oh, sweetie, don't do that on my account. Just kidding! I can't believe how much progress you've made in such a short time. You're really quite fast, even faster than I'd hoped," Marylou said, turning toward the addition.

If she hadn't been looking toward the addition, Jace would have worried that she'd been talking about something else entirely. But that couldn't be. Nobody knew what had happened. How could they? Unless Chessie had— No, she wouldn't say anything. Just like he wouldn't say anything. Just *why* neither of them would say anything he didn't want to dwell on right now.

"We've had a setback, Marylou. Like I told you on the

phone this morning. You really should have a staircase in there, a direct connection between workroom and storage room."

"Oh, and I agree. So does Chessie. She doesn't agree about the alarm system, but she isn't going to fight us on it."

"So, uh, she's not on her way out here?" Had he sounded disappointed? He didn't want to sound disappointed. Except now it was pretty plain that she was avoiding him. "Because, you know," he added quickly, "I thought I could get your opinions on where to place the staircase. There are two possibilities."

Marylou smiled a close-mouth smile—rather like the Cheshire Cat—and shook her head. "Nope. I sent her upstairs to rest. You know, I think she didn't sleep much last night. And look at you. You don't look much better. Why don't I make this easy for you, and we'll pretend I just said yes to everything? Because I really want to help."

Every word Marylou said was innocent. It was just the *way* she said them. And the way her smile kept getting wider.

"Are you sure?"

"Oh yes. Positive. But I doubt you need it. My help, that is. I have every confidence in you, Jace. You've just proved to me that I still know what I'm doing, although I was worried there for a minute, I'll tell you that. I'm sure you'll find a way to work things out." She patted him on the cheek. "Now I'm off to buy something expensive and unnecessary. I feel this need to reward myself. *Ciao!*"

Jace lifted his hand, gave her a fairly weak wave. "Right. *Ciao,*" he said, and then added once she was out of earshot, "Jace, old buddy, you have been *played*. Both of us were played. I wonder if Chessie has figured it out." Then he thought about that for a moment, and decided that he wasn't going to be the one who told her. "This could get interesting."

He unclipped the cell phone from his belt and punched in Carl's number. "Hey, where are you guys heading? Okay, I'll meet you there. Order me two steak sandwiches with the works. Yes, two. Suddenly I'm hungry."

The salon was open Saturday, but the crew constructing the addition clearly worked a five-day week.

Sunday lasted six months, and that was figuring conservatively.

Monday, Chessie woke from the exhausted sleep of the dead to the sound of hammers and electric saws. Music to her ears, even as a knot began to form in the pit of her stomach.

A new week. A new beginning.

She'd spent hours, what seemed like years, thinking about what had happened between Jace and herself. What had started it all, how it had gone wrong.

What had been right about it.

Yes, she'd told him, nearly sworn to it, that she didn't want a relationship. He'd said the same thing.

Poor guy, he'd probably believed that, too. She had.

But what she'd thought was all about the sex hadn't turned out to be all about the sex. Not that there had been anything even the least bit wrong with the sex—she didn't have a whole lot of experience to draw on, but she was pretty sure the man was very, very good at what he did!

Still, it was the night spent talking in the kitchen that she'd thought about most often over the past endless days. His stupid smile. The story about how he'd tried to rescue a cat from a tree when he was twelve, and the fire department had ended up having to rescue him. The way he looked like a fish out of water when confronted with the frillier and more intimate bits of bridal apparel in the shop.

The way he'd played Toby Nieth like a fiddle. That memory got funnier the more she thought about it.

What she and Jace needed to do, what had seemed rational and possible in the dark of last night at least, was for the two of them to start over. Get to know each other. Talk more. See where it led. They'd put the proverbial cart before the horse, that's what they'd done, hopping straight into bed. Now it was time to see if the horse could catch up...or something like that.

Because she missed him. She really, really missed him, and she couldn't forget the hurt and anger in his eyes when she'd tried to be so adult, so *hip,* the morning after they'd been together.

They'd been so...attracted to each other. On such an

immediate and intense level. But now that was out of their systems. She guessed. They wouldn't know if there were anything else they had in common if she hid herself away from him, nerve-racking as it would be to see him again after what they'd done.

But this first meeting? Man, talk about awkward. She really dreaded it. Asking him if they could start over, as friends, would be the most difficult thing she'd ever done, and that included calling all the wedding guests and telling them to enjoy themselves at the reception, because the food and the band were already paid for, but they could just skip the church, as the groom wasn't going to be there.

He could say no, avoid her. But he could just as easily say yes, and they could get to know each other as people, see where it might lead. There was that cart-and-horse thing again.

Because she really did like him. Take away the six-pack, the crazy monkey sex that had been like nothing she'd ever experienced or had even hoped to experience, and she really did like him.

Maybe this time she wouldn't muck it up….

As the hammering and sawing seemed to get louder, she rolled out of bed, yawned and stretched in her thigh-high sleep shirt, and walked into the bathroom with both hands raised to her head, scrubbing at her tangled curls.

Her scream probably was heard in nearby Bethlehem and points east.

"What?" Jace said, looking *way* too happy to be standing in her bathroom with a hammer in his hand, the wall beside the toilet now half-open to the addition. "We were already down to just breaking through the last bit of wall on Friday. Oh, wait. Did I forget to call you? Damn. You know what? I did. I completely forgot to call you. Sorry about that."

"You…you…" She held both hands to her chest, waiting for her heart to start beating again. "*You!* You did that on purpose!"

He walked farther into her bathroom. In his tight jeans and work boots. His tool belt that hung provocatively, like a gunslinger's holster. Not wearing a shirt. His yellow hard hat rakishly tipped over one eye.

Sex on a stick. He was still sex on a stick. And he knew it, damn him!

"You get out of here," she told him, even as she backed up, stupidly tugging at the hem of her sleep shirt. *Yeah, girl, like there's something he hasn't seen yet.* "I have to shower, I have to get ready for work. I've got to brush my teeth and—damn it, Jace, you're standing there looking like one of the Village People, and I have to pee!"

"We all have our little problems," he said, still with that maddening smile on his face. "Tell you what. How about you get me a sheet or a blanket, or something, and I'll tack it up until you're…done. But after that, this bathroom is out of commission for at least three days. Sorry."

"A sheet? You expect me to…with only a…with all of you out there and— Are you out of your tiny mind?"

"You don't like that idea?" Jace slipped the hammer into a loop on his tool belt. "You've got that half bath downstairs."

She was so angry she could barely see straight. "There's no shower in that bathroom. I want to take a shower. *Three days?* You've got to be kidding me!"

"You're right. More like four, probably. We broke through downstairs, too. So, you know, we're going to be in and out. A lot. I know where the linen closet is. Do you want me to get you that sheet?"

"No, I do not want you to get me that sheet," Chessie said, her voice dripping sarcasm. "I want you to go straight to—"

"You're really never a morning person, are you?"

She picked up her liquid-soap dispenser—it was the closest thing to her—and winged it at him. Instead of catching it, Jace stepped neatly to one side and let it go crashing out into the addition, the bisque china shattering on the raw floorboards.

"Why didn't you catch that!" she yelled at him when he grinned. "That was part of a set. It's three years old, and I'll never be able to match it. Now I have to get a whole new— Oh! Just get out of here."

"I don't know, Chess. You've still got that toothbrush-holder thing. Are you sure you don't want to give it another shot? Since it doesn't match anything anymore. I promise not to duck this time."

She turned on her heel and stormed out of the bathroom, heading for the stairs and the powder room below.

"I'm going to hang a heavy canvas tarp," he called after her. "You've got an hour, and then we rip out the shower stall."

She didn't bother answering him. It was only when she was halfway down the stairs that she realized that she'd spent an entire weekend worrying about how awkward it would be when she next saw him. What would she say? What would he say? How uncomfortable would it be?

"At least I don't have *that* to worry about anymore. I think it's safe to say that we've pretty much moved past the awkward stage...."

"Hi, I'm Elizabeth," the very pretty and considerably pregnant woman said, holding out her hand to Jace. "I thought I should ask if you need anything in here moved out of your way."

They were standing in the stockroom, or whatever the area was called. There were long, clear zippered bags suspended everywhere on long metal rods, each one of them holding a wedding gown or some other sort of gown. There were veils, and nearly one wall of shoe boxes and other boxes. There was this frilly thing displayed on a headless mannequin made of birch twigs or some damn thing. It was about the size of a bathing suit, strapless, with lace and long garters he'd been sort of staring at—yeah, they were called garters—hanging from it. A girdle? Nah, something fancier than a girdle. Chessie would look like a million dollars wearing something like that. Not that he'd let her wear it for long.

"Hi, Elizabeth. Jace Edwards," he said, pulling off his leather work glove to shake her hand. "We're pretty good, actually, thank you. I was just thinking about the sawdust factor. I think we can keep it to a minimum, do our cutting mostly outside. But not the noise, I'm afraid, when we frame out this new door. Is that going to be a distraction to your customers?"

"We're not booked too solidly for the next few days, so we'll manage." She stepped through the opening to look at the addition. "Wow, this is larger than I thought it was going to be." She turned in a slow circle, and then frowned.

"Something wrong?"

"No," she said, now tipping her head to one side. "It's just that—is that what's called a weight-bearing wall?" she asked, pointing to what had been the rear exterior wall of the house.

"You could say so. Why?"

"Well, then it doesn't matter, does it? But it would have been really terrific if we could have made this all one huge room instead of two. That way we could extend the hanging bars most of the way on two sides, you know, with the storage on the short walls and in the middle, making it a lot easier to access the gowns. The way we have it now, with row after row of gowns, sometimes when you're in the racks you can feel like you're being swallowed up by the gowns. Right now especially," she said, putting a hand to her belly.

"We could do it," Jace said, eyeing the same weight-bearing wall. "That would give you, oh, roughly thirty-five feet of hanging space on each wall. It wouldn't be cheap," he added, smiling. "There would have to be two posts across the new, wider opening. Yeah, two support posts. And I'd have to have an architect draw up the plans, redo the permit again. The bathroom expansion is already approved, and I've got another new application in for the staircase. But I can see what you mean, I think."

"Marylou would love it, I know she would. She's always complaining about how crowded the gowns are. Let me go get Chessie," Elizabeth said, clearly excited by the prospect. "Can you stay here a minute?"

"Sure." Jace had been hanging out in the stockroom like a stalker anyway, while the crew was on their morning break, hoping to see her. She'd been really funny this morning. And really mad. But at least they were talking again. He'd had a feeling she'd avoid him until the job was over unless he made the first move. Breaking into her bathroom might not have been much on finesse, but it had worked.

Pulling a small spiral notebook from his back pocket, Jace began sketching out the addition and the stockroom, drawing in the existing windows and considering how much free floor space there would be for perhaps a free-standing double-sided shelving area running floor to ceiling, still allowing room for easy maneuvering through the area. Elizabeth had good ideas, but he thought he might be able to improve on them, actually more than double the capacity of the new space.

"Elizabeth said you wanted to see me."

Jace turned around, surprised to see Chessie had come alone.

"She got a walk-in," Chessie said, as if that explained Elizabeth's absence. "So?"

"So?" He smiled, noticing that her hands were balled up into fists. They still had some work to do if they were going to feel comfortable with each other. "How did that work out this morning? For your shower, I mean."

"Okay. But that's it? Now the shower is gone? I didn't know I was getting a new shower stall. Will I like it?"

"It won't be as...cozy as the old one," Jace told her, and watched as color invaded her cheeks—he got a real kick out of her blushes, which probably made him sick and twisted in some way. "But it's a steam shower as well, all glass, no metal framing the edges. And it has a seat. And, uh...lots of showerheads. Body jets, I think they're called. A rain shower. A handheld. Lots...lots of body jets."

"Really?" Chessie seemed to have some difficulty swallowing. "I think I remember Marylou telling me she and Ted had something like that installed at their house last year. She...she, uh, said they're...very nice. I didn't know I was getting all that. When did that happen?"

"Comes with the package," Jace said, speaking with the part of his brain that wasn't busy imagining himself and Chessie in that shower, together. Lingering there, experiencing all the shower had to offer. Adjusting the spray heads from massage, to power spray, to pulsating. Definitely to pulsating. Reclining together on the built-in seat, their bodies all wet and slippery and tingling, while the water...

He probably should talk to her about installing a new, larger water heater.

"Jace?"

He snapped back to attention, realizing he'd been staring at her, and shifted his tool belt so that it hung lower on his waist, the hammer handle hopefully concealing the bulge in his jeans. How the hell was he going to convince her this wasn't all about the sex, that he really wanted to get to know her? As a person.

"Do you want to take a ride? Talk?" he heard himself ask her. "We could...go feed the ducks?"

"Feed the— Well, I guess I..." She looked toward the shop, and then at him. "You're serious?"

She was so beautiful. So vulnerable. He could taste her, feel the silk of her curves against his palms. See her lying naked in the middle of her bed, unashamed, reaching for him, taking him in, taking him deep, taking him to where he'd never been, to experience an intensity of feeling he'd never experienced, bringing him home...

He wanted her so badly he shocked even himself. And then he wanted more; all of her, mind as well as body. "I think it might be better if we stick to public places for a while, don't you? Otherwise, I don't know how much talking we're going to get done."

The corners of her kissable mouth turned up slightly before she nodded. "Sounds like a plan. I'll go get the loaf of bread and a box of crackers from my kitchen."

"And I'll go stick my head under the hose until at least part of me cools off," he muttered once she'd gone.

Chapter Seven

"...Which is when I finally took a chance and started my own company. If Carl believed in me enough to come along for the ride, how could I not believe in myself?"

"And the rest, as they say," Chessie said as she tossed more ripped-up bread toward the impatiently trailing ducks, "is history. How many years ago was that?"

"Not long enough ago that I'm about to repaint the sides of my trucks to add Established in the Year, etc. I don't want to scare off prospective clients."

"You didn't scare off Marylou. She says you have her full confidence. At first I— Never mind."

"No, tell me. We've been doing pretty good so far. Talking, deftly avoiding getting bird droppings on our shoes. I haven't tried to jump your bones— Sorry, that was crude."

"Yes, it was," Chessie said, avoiding his eyes as they walked along the path. "At least you didn't point out that I have also refrained from jumping yours. I think I'll reward myself with two hot dogs instead of one when you take me to lunch across the street."

"They make the best hot dogs in town. Carl can down six in a sitting. My own personal best is five. You thought Marylou what?"

"You're going to keep pushing, aren't you? Okay. I thought Marylou hired you because you're…attractive."

"Just another pretty face, you mean?" he asked, grinning at her.

She looked him up and down, coughed a single time. "For starters, yes." She spied an empty bench. "Can we sit down? I keep thinking I'm going to step on one of these guys."

Chessie sat down first, and Jace sat beside her. Not too close, but not on the other end of the bench, either. They were a…companionable distance apart.

"I think I get the idea," Jace told her, throwing a handful of crackers as far as anyone can reasonably expect to throw crackers, diverting some of the ducks. "Marylou likes men?"

"Now there's an understatement. But she's got one," Chessie said ruefully. "Now she thinks everyone else has to have one, too. You met Elizabeth today. She's married to my cousin Will, partly because of Marylou. Well, and me. We both worked on that one, I'll admit that. But Claire and her husband, Nick, are all Marylou's work. Well, and maybe that was a little me, too—but I only did what Marylou asked me to do. Oh, I'm sorry. You look confused. I'm not saying this right."

"You're saying that Marylou likes to match up people."

"*Likes* might be too tame a word. I think she considers it a calling."

"Okay. So, since Marylou has her man, and there's no one else on the premises she could be playing Cupid for…" He put out his hands and moved them up and down a little, as if weighing two things against each other. "You and me?"

"Yes, but she doesn't know…you know. About…you know."

"Are you sure?"

Chessie looked at him curiously. "Why are you asking that? What did she do? Oh, God, do I really want to hear this?"

"There's nothing to hear. I was just wondering out loud, that's all," Jace said, moving a little closer on the bench, to reach into the bread bag, or at least that would appear to be his reason. "Let me take a guess here. Tennis Anyone was Marylou's work?"

"No, not him. Elizabeth did that one, and she's promised not to do it again. Marylou has someone lined up for next week, though, I do know that. A dinner party, again. I've gotten to really, really hate dinner parties. Next up after that will be Claire, I'm already betting on that one. But it's all because of Marylou, this sudden big push. She thinks I'm still— Never mind."

"You do that a lot."

Chessie looked at him in confusion. "Do what a lot?"

"Say never mind. You start something, and then you say never mind. I'd really like it if you'd just finish whatever it is you were going to say."

"Why? Maybe I stop because I think I might bore you."

He reached out and stroked a single finger down the side of her cheek. "I'll let you know if I get bored, if you'll do the same with me. But I don't think we're in any danger of that yet."

Chessie resisted the strong desire to lean against him, offer up her mouth to him. But it wasn't easy. Kissing Jace was suddenly a lot less dangerous than talking to him.

"My fiancé left me at the altar," she said quickly. "Six years ago."

"I've heard that."

"That's right, I did tell you that, when we were exchanging reasons why we aren't looking for relationships. Did I tell you he and my ex-best friend and maid of honor are now divorced, and that he's back in town? That he called the salon and left a message that he wants to meet for dinner? More than one message. Like maybe six or eight of them?"

"No." Something went hard in Jace's eyes. "I don't

think you told me that. Let me take another shot. Is this jerk-off named Rick?"

Chessie rummaged through her brain for how he could know that, and came up with an answer. "That night in the salon, when I was waiting for Toby. You heard Marylou and me talking. And you heard more than a few words, didn't you?"

He raised his hand. "Guilty as charged. Is she right?"

Chessie emptied the bread bag, shaking out the crumbs at her feet, and then was grateful when Jace took her hand and pulled her up and away from the rapidly advancing ducks. "Thanks. I didn't realize they'd attack like that."

"Uh-huh," he said, keeping hold of her hand as they walked back down the path. "You didn't answer me. Is Marylou right?"

"I didn't return his calls. Does that answer your question?"

"Not really, no. You haven't seen this guy in six years, right? Aren't you at least curious?"

"Do I have to be?" Chessie asked, trying to ignore the nervous fluttering that had begun in her stomach.

"Maybe he's fat and bald. You might enjoy that."

"He is losing his hair a little. Marylou told me."

"There you go. But he's back in town, a onetime loser. Do you know where he's living?"

Chessie nodded, grinning. "He's back home with his mother. That sort of makes him a two-time loser, doesn't it?"

Jace squeezed her hand. "If he doesn't have a job, it's three strikes and he's out."

"He has a job. What he doesn't have is a dinner date with me. And he's not going to." Did she sound vehement? Maybe too vehement?

"He hurt you, Chess. I know the feeling."

They turned and headed up the hill to his pickup. "Your divorce wasn't amicable?"

Jace opened the passenger-side door and put a hand to her elbow to help boost her up onto the high bench seat before walking around the front of the pickup and climbing in behind the wheel.

"Jace? You're not allowed to say never mind, not if I can't."

He put the key in the ignition, but didn't turn it. "Okay," he said, leaning back against the seat, looking out through the windshield but probably seeing something other than the scenery. "Our divorce was…enlightening. And my fault."

"But you said you came home to find your wife in bed with another man."

Jace turned his head to look at her. "You remember that?"

She put her hand on his forearm, feeling the need to comfort him. "I remember everything you've said to me. I said I thought my tale of woe might have topped yours, but at least I escaped being married to someone who'd cheat, who was cheating at the time, as a matter of fact."

"I may have pushed Diana into it. No, scratch that. I did push her into it. I worked long hours, trying to establish my business. I went to night school twice a week and then accelerated college courses all day Saturdays. Sundays I was either studying or doing the business books, or stretched out on the couch, catching up on sleep. I wasn't there, wasn't around even when I was around, you know? I thought she knew why I was working so hard, that there was a goal, a time when all this work would pay off for both of us. It wasn't until the marriage was over that I actually asked myself if I'd ever really asked her if she wanted what I wanted. Because, you know, clearly she wanted something different. Not a husband who was pretty much taking her for granted. I was too tired to take her out on Saturday nights, too busy to sit and watch a TV show with her. Too self-involved, I guess you'd call it."

He shrugged his shoulders, as if shrugging off the memory. "We didn't even make it to our first anniversary. She found somebody else, someone who could give her what she needed. I don't blame her. I wasn't being fair to her."

Chessie nodded, biting her bottom lip, but said nothing for a full minute, waiting for her own pain to pass, she supposed. "I'm sorry. I was just thinking back to when I started Second Chance Bridal. I put everything I had into it, ten days a week, twenty-seven hours a day. I don't know if I would have done that if Rick and I had actually gotten married. It wouldn't have seemed…fair."

Jace gave a short, rueful laugh. "Nice to know you agree with me."

"What? Oh, no. No, I didn't mean it that way. You were trying to build a future for yourself and your wife. That's commendable. Women…women probably just think differently, that's all. We're not often so single-minded that we— No, that's not what I'm trying to say, either. We were raised to be more aware of other people's— Damn it, stop looking at me that way. I'm not saying you were being selfish or thoughtless, I'm really not. What your wife did was terrible. She should have sat you down, talked to you, told you she wasn't getting what she needed from the marriage. Rick should have told me he wanted to at least postpone the wedding, or broken it off sooner."

"Communication. What you're saying here, Chess, is that people don't communicate very well. People who supposedly love each other should be able to communicate with each other."

She sighed heavily. "Yes, that's it. All the fault is never just on one side. Rick, your ex, they should have talked to us. But on the other hand, I should have noticed something was wrong. You should have noticed something was wrong. Why didn't we? Or did we, but we didn't want to acknowledge it?"

"Or maybe we just didn't want to admit to being wrong?"

Chess's smile was quick, but short-lived. "Yeah. That, too. I can be…stubborn. Especially when I want something."

"But you're willing to work for what you want. That's—*commendable* was the word you used. It's a good word."

"You're only saying that to make yourself look good," she teased, squeezing his arm and then finally, reluctantly, drawing back her hand. "The bottom line, Jace, is that both of us have been burned, and both of us know we weren't blameless, that we'd been holding the match too long, or something."

"And neither of us is in a hurry to make a second mistake," he ended, finally turning the key in the ignition. "How about those hot dogs? Confession may be good for the soul, but it doesn't do squat for an empty stomach."

She was glad for the change of subject; things were getting just a little too intense. "I want two. Well done. With mustard and a lot of onions. Someone has destroyed my bathroom, but I can brush my teeth in the kitchen when we get back to the shop."

"A determined man can overlook a few onions, you know," he told her as he eased the truck slowly down the roadway, waiting for a mother duck to herd her babies across to the grass. "Besides, I'm going to have them, too, so they'll sort of cancel each other out."

"I'll ignore that, since we're not going there right now. You don't mind, do you?"

"If I said I did?"

She busied herself taking off her sunglasses and polishing them with the hem of her skirt. "It wouldn't matter.

I mean, it would matter. But it wouldn't matter. We're being smart."

"We're being something," Jace agreed, looking left, right and left again, before pulling across the four lanes of Hamilton Boulevard.

"Yes, looking both ways before proceeding cautiously," Chessie told him. "So far so good?"

He grinned at her, and something inside her, some nervous knot in the region of her stomach, relaxed and slid back to where it was supposed to be. "Yeah. So far so good. But let's not let Marylou know, okay?"

"Oh, you can count on that. I'm certainly not telling her. Let her run in circles for a while."

"Nasty. I like that in a woman. Let's eat."

Wednesday afternoon Marylou slid into the diner booth and looked across the table at coconspirators Elizabeth and Claire. "She's glowing," she announced without preamble, and in a tone usually reserved for delivering news of the really, really bad sort.

"Oh, no," Elizabeth said. "How could she?"

Claire put down her fork as if she'd suddenly lost her appetite for the Cobb salad on her plate. "I can't believe it. Wasn't getting hurt once enough for her? How could she be seriously considering going back to him?"

"There *have* been developments. I couldn't get to you two because I had this charity dinner thing with Ted, and some other stuff. She's definitely got something going on. *But* I don't think it's Rick," Marylou told them, motioning to the waitress and then smiling and pointing to Claire's salad, wordlessly ordering a duplicate for herself. "I mean, I can't be sure, it's just a hunch. But I do know it isn't Toby Nieth."

"He was a total failure," Elizabeth agreed sorrowfully. "Even I cringed when I saw him with that dumb sweater tied around his shoulders. He didn't even take it off during dinner. I kept waiting for one of the sleeve ends to plop into the tomato sauce. Will said if it had, Toby would probably have sent us the dry-cleaning bill."

Marylou waved her hands in front of her, figuratively erasing Toby Nieth. "Just forget him. You tried, and that's wonderful."

"We can forget him," Claire said, "but we have to remember that Chessie tried to use him to cover up who she's really seeing. Her ex-fiancé. Except you just said she isn't. I think. What exactly are you saying, Marylou?"

"That I'm sure, but not sure. She let me think she's seeing Rick, and we're going to have a small discussion about that someday. Just not now, because I think—no, I'm almost positive—I know who she's really seeing." Marylou looked to her right, as if to make sure nobody was standing close enough to the booth that she could be overheard. "I think she and our contractor...indulged themselves last week. And I mean big-time. *Big. Time.*"

"Oh, Marylou," Elizabeth said on a sigh. "Chessie wouldn't do that. Not with someone she barely knows. She's not like that."

"I agree with Elizabeth, Marylou. Chessie isn't the fall

into bed at the drop of a hat—hammer—type. It has to be Rick, someone she knows. That's just wishful thinking on your part, that it's this contractor. Although why anyone would wish Chessie would do something that dangerous and impulsive is pretty much beyond me. She would never go for a one-night stand with a near stranger. Not Chessie."

"She fell into bed with somebody. Not that she looked too happy about it the next day, when she admitted it to me. Well, she didn't deny it, anyway. But I've got eyes. Then she got all down and depressed, which I assumed meant she'd had second thoughts, but then when I saw her yesterday she was all up and bubbly again. So my guess is they've decided to make it more than a one-night stand. Not that she'll tell me anything. I swear to you, the woman has turned into a clam. She denies now that she's seeing anyone, just as if last week never happened. But she's happy, glowing, bordering on nauseatingly cheerful. So, you know, something's *definitely* going on."

"What is this guy like? The contractor? Is he married, or something? Is there a reason she's not talking? Nick could look through the archives or whatever they are down at the newspaper office, check him out."

"Oh, I already did that," Marylou said off-handedly, and then sort of ducked her head.

"Marylou Smith-Bitters—is this contractor your contribution to The Bride Plan? Because if he is, you didn't tell us. Is that playing fair, Claire?" Elizabeth asked.

"All's fair in love and The Bride Plan, I guess," Claire

said, shrugging. "What's the matter, Marylou? You didn't want to tell us, just in case your plan went belly-up?"

"All right, yes. I'm trying to keep my batting average up. It's pretty high now, thanks to you and Nick, Claire, and I didn't want to lower it with another Chessie failure. There have been so many."

Elizabeth had been silent for a while, deep in thought. "Or this is all happening without your interference, and you figure if you get a claim in now, you can still get points. Keep your average up. That would be really sneaky of you, Marylou."

"It would," Marylou said as the waitress put the Cobb salad in front of her, "except that I did pick Jace Edwards out personally. Not that he isn't a great contractor, but the other contractors on my list of potential choices for the expansion all bit the dust when I saw Jace. He was perfect for the job."

"Which one?" Claire asked, winking at Elizabeth. "The addition, or for finding a match for Chessie? I'm hoping you weren't just trying to hook her up with a bed partner, at least."

"Sometimes you two don't appreciate all my hard work," Marylou said, stabbing a forkful of salad. "And before we all get too happy, remember that I said I *thought* Chessie and Jace were…you know. But I can't be one-hundred-percent positive she isn't tricking me into thinking what I'm thinking so that I stop thinking about Rick Peters. So The Bride Plan goes on. We keep introducing her to new men, just in case she *is* seeing Rick. So she has others to compare him to, like your doctor friend, Claire. She'd need to see the error of her ways, going back with that scumbag."

"Oh. Must we?"

Marylou put down her fork and looked at the two women seriously (or as seriously as her half-frozen facial muscles would allow). "It's either that, ladies, or we stage an intervention."

Elizabeth groaned, and then quickly flagged down their waitress. "I'll have a slice of the blueberry-topped cheesecake, please. And one for my friend."

After allowing the new white subway tile on the shower-stall walls to rest for two days, the grout to dry completely, Jace had come upstairs at quitting time to test the new shower system. He entered the enlarged bathroom through the door that led to the workroom and then stopped to admire what they'd accomplished in five short days.

Marylou had given him carte blanche to design and outfit the bathroom any way he wanted, which was surprising. But then again, it wasn't Marylou's bathroom, and since Chessie hadn't asked any questions, it had been quicker to just pick everything on his own.

He couldn't be sure, no man could ever be sure, but he thought he had a fairly good handle on what Chessie would like. He probably should ask himself why he thought about her to the point of getting inside her head and trying to think like her, but the answer would probably make him nervous.

Still, he prided himself on the fact that he'd found replacement fixtures that managed to be functionally modern, yet still had a decidedly Victorian look to them, in keeping with the age and style of the house. Even the one-inch black-and-white tile on the floor was consistent with the era.

Chessie's soap dish and toothbrush holder, however, wouldn't have matched anyway, not with their beige tones and small pink roses stuck to the sides, and the smashed liquid-soap dispenser had to be replaced in any case.

So he'd done a little retail shopping of his own last night at one of the department stores in the mall. Not that he'd gotten too far before one of the salesclerks came to his rescue and pointed him in all the right directions. Men don't belong in malls, that was Jace's thought on the subject of shopping. Yet, for Chessie, he'd done it.

He probably shouldn't think too much about that, either.

He opened the bag he'd brought with him and took out the soap dish, toothbrush holder and liquid-soap dispenser he'd picked up last night, and lined them up on the black granite sink surround. Each piece was made of some bumpy white glass the salesclerk had called hobnail, and with silver accents that matched the chrome on the faucets, towel bars and everything else his guilt had made him toss into the purchase and the crew had installed earlier that morning. Even a new, mirrored wastebasket the clerk had told him, "Your wife will just love."

He was having some second thoughts, since the bathroom was now strictly a black-and-white affair, but he figured Chessie could do something girly and feminine with the towels and stuff, and that would make it all right.

Taking out his punch list, he checked to make sure Carl had touched up the paint around the original-to-the-house stained-glass window and attached the baseboard-mounted doorstoppers, and then turned to escape before Chessie happened to come upstairs and catch him leaving his presents.

He felt nervous about giving her presents, not sure how she'd react. She'd seemed thrilled with the flowers he brought her last night, when they'd played Scrabble while watching the Phillies game; not so thrilled with the way he'd turned her word *ion* into *seduction*.

She'd said it was because he'd managed to spell it using a Triple Word Score block, but he wasn't so sure about that.

But how could he help it? When they were in her living room, all he could think about was the way she'd turned to him that night, untying the strings to her halter top.

When they'd gone into the kitchen for more of Berthe's peanut-butter-and-chocolate-chip cookies, he'd looked at the kitchen table and remembered how they'd— No, not smart to revisit that memory again for a while.

And when he'd walked through her bedroom on his

way to use the nearly finished bathroom, just the sight of that big brass bed had damn near had him breaking every resolution he'd thought he could keep.

Looking at the new shower stall, the new showering system, imagining the two of them in that shower, trying out all the different body jets?

Torture above and beyond endurance, that's what that was.

But, hey, they'd agreed. They'd put the cart before the horse. Leaped before they'd looked. And something else… Oh, yeah, run before they'd walked.

Wednesday night, when they'd met at the local cineplex and shared popcorn and a mediocre movie before saying good-night in the parking lot, she'd even had the nerve to wink at him and tell him that good things come to those who wait.

It was only on his way home that he'd thought up a comeback for that one: *He who hesitates is lost.*

Not to mention frustrated. Teeth-grindingly, cold-shower-takingly frustrated.

He'd never felt this way. Never.

Friends was good. Learning about each other was good.

Remembering how they'd been together that night was torture.

But he'd move at Chessie's pace. Not that he had a choice. Not that he wanted a choice, he guessed. One-time losers didn't have the luxury of leaping before they looked. Looked really hard, and long, and made damn sure they weren't heading for loss number two.

But, damn…

"Oh, look at this. It's gorgeous!"

"Ah, we meet again, back at one of the scenes of the crime. The leaper and the leap-ee. Steady man," Jace murmured under his breath before turning to watch Chessie enter the bathroom, slowly walking around the fairly large space, touching things.

She looked so good, dressed in an aqua-blue-and-yellow filmy flowered skirt and a light green sweatery thing that had a V-neck and tiny pearl buttons running down the front of it. Professional, yet touchable. Chessie was eminently touchable.

She picked up the liquid-soap dispenser, turned it in her hands. "Oh, my goodness. Hobnail milk glass. They still make this? My grandmother used to have a tea set made in this design. We'd use it on special occasions, just her and me and a couple of my dolls. I'll never be able to look at these pieces without thinking of my nana. Did you buy these for me? *Thank you,* Jace."

She put the dispenser down and wrapped her arms around his shoulders, pressing a kiss on his cheek.

He shoots, he scores, Jace thought as he wound his arms around her waist and pulled her closer. Although it was odd. Pleased as he was to have Chessie in his arms again, he felt happier to have made her happy.

That probably wasn't a good sign for a guy who wasn't looking for a long-term relationship.

"Oh, good Lord, Jace," Chessie said, looking over his shoulder. "I purposely stayed away, but now that I can see the shower? Am I going to need an engineering degree to figure out all those knobs and levers?" She moved away from him to cautiously approach the glass doors.

"I studied the manual last night," he told her, taking hold of her shoulders and gently moving her to one side so he could open the wide door. "See this? That's your all-in-one, handy-dandy control system. With this, you can control the different showerheads, select the steam shower version, choose the music, start the light show."

She slipped out of her shoes and stepped past him, right into the shower, her head forward on her neck as if this would help her see what she obviously couldn't believe she was seeing. "Music? I'll have music in the shower?" She turned quickly to face him. "Did you say *lights?*"

Jace pulled off his work boots before stepping into the shower, and then reached past her and activated the light system. "It's for ambiance, or so I read in the manual. Let's see here. Okay, here we go. We can do sunrise or sunset, partly cloudy with a chance of showers—"

"Oh, come on, you've got to be kidding me."

She had her hand against his back now. He'd been right. They'd both fit. Really well.

"Nope. And, last but not least, this one gives you a light reflection that looks like water, water, everywhere. Hey, that's not too bad."

"Go back to sunset. I think I like that one best."

Chessie was beginning to get into this, he could tell. "Is there any music loaded in this thing? Can I load in some of my favorites? I mean, for some reason that old Eddie Rabbitt song 'I Love a Rainy Night' is running through my head. I can't wait to try all of this, I really can't."

Sometimes you plan ahead. Think. Strategize. Execute.

And then sometimes maybe the Devil just makes you do it….

"I don't know that one. I was thinking more of another oldie but goody, 'Raindrops Keep Falling on My Head,'" Jace said just as he pushed the button that activated the two huge rain showerheads above them.

Chessie let out a high-pitched yelp as they were both instantly soaked, and Jace grabbed her, holding her close against him until the water quickly went from ice-cold to pleasingly warm.

She managed to push herself slightly away from him, looking up at him, her hair plastered to her head, her clothes wonderfully plastered to her body. "Are you insane? I'm on my dinner break. I have to go back downstairs in an hour."

Jace shook his head to get some of the water out of his eyes. "You said you couldn't wait to try it out," he reminded her, wondering if he should duck.

"Oh, hell," she said, pleasing him even more than he thought she could, "as long as we're here, huh? I can't get any wetter. What else does this monster machine do?"

"I'm so glad you asked," he said, and really meant

it. He turned her to face the controls. "We have lights, we have the preloaded demo music—I've always liked Beethoven's Ninth, haven't you?—and we have the rain showers. Please note, directly above you, the handheld shower spray, convenient for washing those areas you may be interested in favoring with special attention. Like so…"

He activated the handheld and directed it at Chessie's hair, so that she tilted her head back and let the shower-head neatly water-comb all her hair back away from her face.

"Nice," she said, leaning her head back farther, so that it rested against his chest, water from the rain shower sluicing off her perfect features. She opened her mouth, let water run into it and then spit it out in a small fountain, grinning at him. "You're still insane. But nice. Is that it?"

"No, Ms. Burton, we're not quite finished with our demonstration," he told her, replacing the handheld, knowing he'd barely begun to demonstrate its uses…or at least the ones he'd thought up last night, while reading the manual. "One last feature. The water jets, body jets. Turn around again."

She looked at him curiously for a moment, but then did what he asked, and he pushed the control button that activated the ten "strategically placed" water jets, plus the control that allowed the water to be recirculated, to conserve that resource. There were two jets at each of five levels: neck, chest, stomach, groin, thighs. Well, depending on the person's height. No matter what, they were some pretty interesting water jets.

"Ohhh," Chessie moaned; he was pretty sure it was a reasonably pleased moan. "It's like having a full-body massage. And the water hits the small of my back just perfectly. Do you know how great that's going to be after I've been sitting cross-legged on the floor for a couple of hours, hot-glue-gunning wedding favors?"

That wasn't the sort of relaxation he'd had in mind, but he was glad she could see practical uses for the shower system. Now to show her what else it could do....

As she stood there, eyes closed, her arms hanging loosely at her sides, enjoying the pulse of the jets against her back, Jace began working on those tiny pearl buttons on her sweater. If she noticed, she didn't say anything. Didn't move.

Not even when he undid the front closure on her bra. Although she may have sighed....

Elastic waistbands hadn't ever been something he'd given much thought to, but he had a great appreciation for the way they made it simple to hook his thumbs behind this one and slide the filmy skirt down past Chessie's hips, beyond the soaked and now nearly transparent silk bikini panties she wore.

"We shouldn't be doing this," she told him as she struggled to slip his buttons through the wet denim of his work shirt. "How are we ever going to learn if we're compatible if we keep doing things like this?"

"You want to stop?"

"Nobody likes a smart-ass, Jace," she said. But she was touching him intimately as she said the words.

She stepped out of her skirt and kicked it to one side, soon to be joined by his work jeans and underwear. Jace retained just enough functioning brain cells to look down and make sure their clothing wasn't clogging the drain, and then allowed himself to be distracted by the way the water ran down Chessie's chest, causing her nipples to harden provocatively. She had the most beautiful breasts he'd ever seen. And they fit his hands perfectly.

He leaned down and kissed her, thrusting his tongue deep inside her mouth as he pinched her nipples between thumb and forefinger and she dug her fingertips into his shoulders, ground her body against his erection.

"Turn around," he murmured against her mouth.

"I… What?"

"Turn around, Chessie," he repeated, dragging his hands over her hips as she slowly turned to face the water jets.

"Oh…."

She leaned against him for support and he looked down at her as the jetting water found her, teased her. He adjusted a few of the jets and then took her hands and told her to cup her breasts.

"Yes. Like that. So that the water hits them. Pulses against them. Teases them. Yes…you like that?"

"I like that…."

"I like watching you when you're feeling good. I want you to feel good. That's what this is all about, Chess.

What I want for you." He slid his hands down over her belly and inside her bikini panties, and touched her intimately as she spread her legs, still bracing against him, the warm water of the shower unable to match the liquid heat of her.

"This is… But what about you, this isn't fair to… *Oh, Jace. Oh, yes. Yes!*"

His own explosion rocked him as he pressed himself against the delightful dip at the small of her back, as all the building tension of the past week was washed away for both of them.

She turned to him once more and they held each other, just held on, as their pulses slowed, as the warm water soothed, relaxed.

He lowered his arm behind her knees and picked her up, turning off the shower and stepping out onto the tiles before putting her down. "There's no towels," he said in dawning comprehension as he looked around the room. "I should have bought towels."

Chessie leaned her forehead against his shoulder and giggled. "At least that shows you didn't plan this. I mean, what just happened wasn't premeditated or anything."

He dropped a kiss on the top of her head. "You just keep thinking that, Chess. I'll be safer that way."

She lifted her head and he was treated to the sight of her gorgeous cornflower eyes opened wide. "We had an arrangement. We agreed…"

"I thought we were agreeing pretty well a couple of minutes ago," he said as she pushed past him to the linen closet and grabbed two large bath towels, tossing one of them at him before wrapping the other around herself and heading for the bedroom. "Chess?" he said, following her after drawing the towel around his waist, tucking in one end. "Physical intimacy is a form of compatibility, right? Just another step in getting to know each other? You're not going to go all woman on me now, are you?"

The moment those last words were out of his mouth he wished them back. Carl's wife, Millie, was so right; men just didn't have a clue, did they?

"You...*you!* Oh, just get out of here, all right? I've got to get dressed and go back to work." She was grabbing clothes and trying to get them onto her still fairly wet body, her hair dripping water down her face.

This probably wasn't the time for a reality check, but he was already into it up to his neck anyway, so he said, "I don't have any other clothes, Chess. I have to toss what I've got into your dryer. Uh—where's your clothes dryer?"

Her grin bordered on evil. No, actually, it went beyond evil, and then passed through diabolical and came out the other side, all the way to *Gotcha!*

"In the basement. The one you have to access by walking through the hallway downstairs. Where Missy is working until I get back. Kind of awkward, huh? You have fun with that, Jace."

Grabbing the towel once more, along with her brush, she left the bedroom, clearly heading downstairs, just as clearly leaving him to figure out his next move.

Well, there was the second door from the bathroom to the workroom. And the new stairs had been installed just today. His pickup was parked in the alleyway, where nobody would really see him.

He'd never tried to put on wet jeans before, but he guessed there was a first time for everything....

Chapter Eight

"There's just that one more long flat box of favors still upstairs, Missy, if you'd please get it for me," Chessie said as she headed for her office and the ringing phone. Elizabeth was in the dressing room with their first client of the morning, and Marylou was already at the bride's house to direct the photographer and videographer, and they had to be set up for the Youngston-Duncan wedding by noon, plus she had to meet the bakery delivery guy at the reception hall in forty-five minutes and the florist right after that. What a morning!

"Already got it, Chessie. All the favors are in the back of your SUV."

"Great. Then how about you grab the plastic fountain in the hall closet. And don't forget the blue food coloring we need for the water. Oh, damn," she said as the phone kept ringing. It was time to face facts: they needed another employee, especially with the wedding-planner part of the business beginning to take off and Elizabeth going on maternity leave next week. "I'm coming, I'm coming— Hello? I mean, Second Chance Bridal and Wedding Planners, may I help you?"

"Chessie? That is you, isn't it?"

Chessie closed her eyes as she sagged against the edge of the desk. Why hadn't she looked at the caller-identification screen before she'd picked up? But it had been so long since he'd called, she'd thought for sure that he'd given up. Why hadn't he given up?"

"Hello, Rick," she said dully. "Yes, it's me. I. Never mind. How…um, how are you?"

"Fine, I guess. But wondering why you haven't called me back. I've left about a dozen messages in the past couple of weeks."

"You have?" Chessie made a mental note to roast Marylou over an open fire. Why hadn't she warned her that Rick was still calling? "Well, gee. I'm, you know, pretty busy?"

"Busy avoiding me—not that I blame you. You know I'm back in Allentown for good? Uh, Diana and me? It didn't work out, Chess."

Chessie rolled her eyes. "Gosh. I'm so sorry to hear that. I mean, with the two of you so obviously well suited to each other." *Both of you backstabbing, rotten, no-good sons-of— Leave it alone, Chessie, leave it alone! You're over it!* "Look, Rick, I'm really busy right now, so—"

"I want to see you, Chess," Rick said, which was just what she'd thought he was going to say and she was trying to avoid having to hear. "We've got some unfinished business, don't you think?"

"No. I think it's pretty finished. I don't think it gets more finished than walking out on somebody the day of the wedding."

"I'm not the same person I was six years ago, Chess. I've changed."

"Good for you. Really, I mean that. Sincerely. But I really have to—"

"Let me apologize, Chessie. I know I'm asking a lot, but I need to do this. I'm not going to make any demands on you, or even ask for your forgiveness. I don't deserve forgiveness for what I did to you. I just need to apologize. Face-to-face. We could meet for dinner tonight. I could pick you up at the salon. I've driven past it a couple of times, but I didn't want to just walk in on you. Please, Chess."

Missy stuck her head into the office, her lower jaw moving and her bubble gum popping. "All set. You ready to leave? It's almost ten-thirty."

Chessie nodded, shooing the teenager with her hand. "Rick, I really have to go now. I've got a noon wedding to pull off and a time schedule to keep. Maybe some other—"

"I won't hang up until you say yes, Chessie. I can pick

you up at seven. I'll make reservations at our—that is, at Lily's."

"Lily's went out of business three years ago, Rick," she told him. He'd been about to say "at our restaurant." Where he'd taken her on their first date. Where he'd proposed. Where they'd had their rehearsal dinner and he'd kissed her good-night in Lily's parking lot while Diana watched and then the two of them had gone flying off to Mexico, leaving her in the lurch, for crying out loud. She didn't know whether to scream at him or to cry. What she should do was hang up on him.

"Really? Well, maybe that's a good thing. It was stupid of me to even suggest it. We'll go somewhere else, some-place new I've never even heard about. Look, Chess, I know you don't owe me anything, but I'm staying here in Allentown, and we're going to run into each other at some point. That could be really awkward. I think it would be best for both of us if we get this first meeting out of the way."

"Chessie? Can I start the car? I've got my Junior License now, you know. Just last week."

Chessie glared at Missy, who was once again lean-ing her head inside the office. "All right. No—not you, Missy, I didn't mean you!" she corrected hurriedly as Missy grinned and turned to run to the car. Could her morning get any worse? "Sorry, Rick. But I guess you've made your point. Seven o'clock tonight. I'll see you then. Goodbye."

She put down the phone and picked up her purse,

took a frustrating ten seconds to locate her file on the Youngston-Duncan wedding and headed for the back door via the new addition.

And stopped dead when she saw Jace standing in the still-uncompleted space, his tape measure out as he measured an already-built shelf attached to the center island. He was dressed in a navy blue T-shirt and khaki shorts and sneakers, wore no tool belt, looked good enough to eat with a spoon, and if he thought he was fooling her into thinking he was here to work then he should probably give some serious thought to acting lessons.

"It's Saturday. What are you doing here? And let's save time here. You're not working."

"True. I was just thinking maybe we could go to lunch later, but Missy already told me you've got a wedding today."

"I told you that yesterday, when we were having dinner," she reminded him. They were back to meeting in public places where, as he'd originally said, it was safer. They'd talked all through dinner, and for an hour afterward, strolling together in the park. He'd held her hand, and only kissed her good-night when he'd walked her to her car. He was being so good since the incident in the shower that her teeth were beginning to hurt.

"Was that before or after we decided who should run for president?"

Why did she let him get to her? He always got to her, just like her brother Sean had always been able to get to their mother, just by grinning at her. She always got into trouble and tried to argue her way out, but not Sean. He'd just grin and say, "I love you, Mom," and the next thing anyone knew, he was off scot-free and out playing with his friends again. He was still pulling the same stunt in Arizona, where he lived with his wife, Jill, and their three kids. Jill complained about it all the time, and kept falling for the same trick. It must be a boy thing, which grew into a man thing. Women just didn't stand a chance.

"Don't grin at me," she told Jace now, trying to be stern. "And it was before we decided who should run for president, and after we'd agreed that limited use of instant replay is good for baseball."

He grinned again.

Damn him…

"Oh, right, I remember now. How about we change it to dinner, instead? What time do you get back from the wedding?"

"It's only a small reception immediately following the— Never mind. I can't, Jace. I already have dinner plans."

"Another of Marylou's setups? Chess, maybe it's time you told her we're seeing each other. It might take a little of the pressure off you. Unless you like blind dates? Oh, and if I sound jealous, please pretend you didn't notice. I'm just being a man."

She didn't answer him directly. It was safer that way. Besides, this was going to be a once and done thing with Rick, a necessary evil to get them both beyond the past and moving into the future. Separately.

"I'll think about it," she said, addressing only his second question. "But if I do that, get ready for the third degree from Marylou about your intentions. Are you ready for that? Because I'm not sure if we're ready for that yet."

Jace stepped closer to her and lifted her chin, pressed a quick, hard kiss against her mouth before stepping back. "I don't know, Chess. I look into those big blue eyes, and I have a lot of trouble remembering why we began putting ourselves through this whole thing in the first place. I think I know how I feel."

Chessie wanted to weep. He'd said just the right thing, and exactly what she'd been thinking. But he'd said it at exactly the wrong time. Which, coincidentally, also wasn't the right time to tell him she was having dinner with Rick tonight.

"Chessie?"

Chessie turned about to look at Elizabeth, who was standing in the doorway. Shipwrecked sailors didn't look at their rescuers with any more hope in their eyes.

"Yeah, Elizabeth? Is something wrong?"

"You could say that. Marylou just called. It seems when she picked up the tuxedos yesterday she forgot to double-check the order. She's frantic, apologizing like crazy, poor thing. Anyway, the groom's tux is still at the shop. You're to run by and pick it up on your way to the church because Marylou can't leave the bride."

"No, she can't. The rental shop is only a couple of blocks out of my way. All right, call her and tell her I've got it under control." Chessie turned back to Jace, who looked so good, so wonderful. She wanted to tell him the same thing he'd just told her. "Jace—"

"I know, you've got to go. I'll call you tomorrow."

She nodded, looked over her shoulder to see that Elizabeth was still standing in the doorway and looking at Jace curiously, as if trying to come to some sort of decision.

"Pretend I just kissed you goodbye, okay?" she whispered to Jace.

"I'll pretend you just kissed me twice," he answered, pulling her car keys from his back pocket and dangling them in front of her. "I intercepted Missy on her way out the back door."

"Thank you," Chessie said fervently, wondering why she didn't just say to hell with it and throw her arms around him, and forget all this stuff about looking and leaping.

She also wondered who she was kidding, pretending she didn't know that this was the man for her, the one man who made her feel alive, and cherished, and most important, *understood*. He knew what it was like to be hurt, to feel responsible, to need to feel certain that the time and the person and the reasons were all *right*. He knew how she felt about her business, because he felt the same way about his. He understood her drive to succeed. He knew how lonely that success could be without someone to share it with.

But then she remembered Rick, and how it probably would be a good idea to see him first in a controlled setting, rather than just running into him somewhere, which would be even more awkward. Old business, she needed to take care of old business. Then it would be on to new business. On to Jace and what they could have together. Jace might not understand that sort of reasoning. It was better he never knew. Easier.

She grabbed the keys and took off for the SUV at a run.

And she kept running for the next eight hours, she and Marylou both. Arranging the favors on the tables at the reception hall. Arranging the fresh greens around the cake. Racing to the church with the groom's tuxedo, and then deftly snatching the bottle of Scotch from the already half-lit best man who was a basket case about having to give the toast and promising him she'd put it in the stretch limo for after the ceremony.

She'd bribed the flower girl with a five-dollar bill that convinced the little blond cherub that it would be all right to toss the rose petals in her basket as she went down the aisle, where her mommy would be waiting for her with the money. It might not be good child psychology, but it usually worked.

She fluffed the veil and gown train, repositioned flowers the bridesmaids were holding as if they were basketballs and posed the wedding party for photographs. She bustled the bride's gown once the receiving line was completed, and chased down the groom's godparents, who had somehow gotten lost in the three miles between the church and the reception hall.

She'd arranged the gifts, watched the money cards like a hawk without looking as if she was, and wiped the bride's chin after her new husband got a little too energetic about feeding his new wife a bite of wedding cake.

She'd draped a cloth napkin over the best man's head as he drooped his head on his arms at the head table and began snoring, happily inebriated, halfway through the dancing.

And then it was over and she and Marylou stayed behind to gather up the pillars and dividers for the wedding cake that had been made up of two hundred cupcakes, to return the equipment to the bakery on Monday morning. She disassembled the fountain, checked under skirted tables and collected two pairs of ladies' shoes, one bow tie and a rather lovely silver charm bracelet somebody was going to start missing sooner or later.

"What do we do about him?" Marylou asked, as the best man was still under cover, and still snoring. "I think they forgot him."

Happily, one of the groomsmen appeared at that point and the best man was soon on his way to his hotel and his Sunday morning hangover, leaving the two women with the feeling of another job well-done and the two cupcakes they'd earlier stashed behind the bar along with two cans of soda.

Marylou took a bite of cupcake, closing her eyes in appreciation of the deep chocolate flavor and creamy white icing. "Yummy. We have to use this bakeshop again, definitely. So, how much did we net?"

"So glad you asked that question, Marylou," Chessie told her, slipping off her high-heel sandals and resting her bare feet on a pulled-out chair. She quoted her partner a figure, and then added, "I think we can safely say we're at the point where we can afford to hire some help. Unless you enjoy spending all your Saturdays doing this, because I need to be at the shop at least two Saturdays a month. It's one of our biggest sell days."

"She starts Monday," Marylou told her. "Carl says she's been complaining about an empty nest for three years, and she's got a retail background. See? And you think I don't notice things."

"Clearly *I* don't. Who's Carl? Oh, wait—do you mean Carl the carpenter? The one who works with—that is, one of the men building the addition?"

"One and the same. Her name's Mildred but she prefers Millie, and she got positively giddy when I told her she'd be working with brides. Turns out she's a real wedding junkie, watches all those shows on TV about brides and gowns and all that stuff. Oh, and she does crafts and scrapbooking, and thinks fussing with bows and glue guns is fun, if you can believe that."

Chessie was dumbfounded, which she knew she shouldn't be. Marylou was always doing something like this, finding just the right person for just the right spot. Still, she had to ask: "How do you do it?"

"I *talk* to people, Chessie," Marylou answered reasonably. "I listen to them, and then I help them. Carl was on his cell phone one day last week when I went outside to look at the new siding—which matches perfectly, if you haven't noticed it yet, Jace is a genius—and he seemed upset when he ended the call, so I asked him what was wrong. Carl, that is, not Jace."

"Uh-huh. Go on, this is fascinating."

"Yes, I know. Anyway, he—Carl, not Jace, because Jace isn't married—said his wife is always asking him when he's coming home because she's alone all day now that the kids are grown, yadda yadda, and he wished she'd find something to do because she's really too young to just sit around waiting for him, and she loves her grand-kids but she raised her kids and she's not too hot on doing the diaper thing again, and— Do I really have to go on here?"

"No, never mind," Chessie told her, slipping her feet into her heels once more. She bent and gave Marylou a kiss on the cheek. "You're one of a kind, Marylou, and I love you. Other than that, I should just learn to stop asking questions. Are you ready to go?"

"Hmm, yes," her friend said, looking at her diamond-studded wristwatch. "Wow, almost six-thirty already? I'm meeting Ted at the club for drinks and a late dinner. How about you? Do you want to come along?"

Chessie turned to head for the parking lot; it was safer lying to Marylou if her friend couldn't see her. "No thanks, I'm beat. I'm just going to go home, let the water jets unkink my back muscles and eat a sandwich in front of the TV."

"You live such a glamorous life. Don't forget the dinner party next week, kiddo. One way or another, we're going to save you from yourself."

Marylou's parting shot kept replaying in Chessie's head as she drove back to the salon, arriving with only ten minutes to spare before Rick showed up. Which was probably a good thing, because racing through brushing her teeth and freshening her makeup kept her from getting too nervous about what it would be like to see her ex-fiancé for the first time in six years.

In fact, she had no time at all, because the doorbell was ringing while she was still pulling a comb through her hair. She physically flinched, dropped the comb and went racing for the stairs, practically sliding across the reception-area floor so that he wouldn't have to ring again and wonder if she'd decided to stand him up, which would be—*just what he deserved,* she thought as she turned on her heel and headed toward her office. Where she stood, trying to control her breathing, until he'd rung the bell a second time.

Some people, she knew, might call her petty for doing such a thing. But she'd bet none of those some people were women.

"Hi," she said as she opened the door, standing back to allow Rick to enter her space. Because it was her space. She'd built it, she'd grown it; this was hers.

"Hi, yourself. You look great, haven't changed a bit," he said, and then he bent and kissed her on the cheek.

Which she certainly hadn't been expecting.

"You, too," Chessie said weakly, looking at him but trying hard to not appear as if she was taking some sort of inventory.

He still wore his dark blond hair in the same carefully shaggy style—she'd have to try to remember to get a good look at the back of his head at some point. His eyes were still the same mix of blue and green with hints of gold—he'd always had fascinating eyes; they were what had first drawn her to him. He was still a good six inches taller than her. *Duh, Chessie, did you think he'd shrink?*

He still wore the watch she'd given him their first Christmas together. If he'd worn it during his marriage, no wonder he and Diana had parted ways; she'd been shopping with Chessie when she'd bought the thing. So, no. He'd probably dug it out of a drawer just for tonight, which was really tacky.

"So this is your place," Rick said, taking a slow walk around the reception area. "My mother told me about it."

Your mother told me it was all my fault that you jumped ship, that her precious baby wouldn't have done something so terrible if I hadn't forced you into it. The old bat. Only thing good about the whole mess was not getting her as my mother-in-law. "Really? How is your mother?"

Rick smiled at her. "You know my mother. The same as always, just more so. She sends her love, by the way."

I'll just bet she does. "How nice. Tell her I said hello. So—ready to go?"

Rick escorted her to his car, which looked eerily the same as Toby Nieth's, and held the door open as she got in, fastened her seat belt.

"Fasten your seat belt, Rick," she told him out of old habit as he slid in behind the driver's seat. He never wore his seat belt, had sixteen different arguments as to why it was safer to not wear a seat belt. They're argued about that more than once. Strange how it was easier to recall the bad times than the good ones.

"We're only going a couple of miles, Chess," he said with the same reasonableness that had caused the arguments.

But that was six years ago. Now was now. She simply shrugged. "Your funeral. Where are we going?"

"I made reservations at an Italian place my mother told me about. It's in a shopping center, but she says the food is very authentic."

Adele Peters was of German and Irish descent and all her best recipes had either potatoes or dumplings as one of the top ingredients. "Well," Chessie said cheerfully, "she should know."

Things didn't get a whole lot better when they arrived at the restaurant and Rick ordered for her without asking her first. A white wine on the rocks. She hadn't had white wine in three years, having discovered a preference for blush wine. And not on the rocks.

She watched him as he ordered his own drink, and then their appetizers and entrées, again, without asking her. That he'd ordered her favorites did nothing to make her feel in charity with him. Instead of going all gooey that he'd remembered her preferences from six years ago, as he might hope, she was tempted to ask him if he thought she couldn't think for herself.

Still, remembering back over their time together, she realized she had let him take charge, had rather enjoyed the way he'd treated her as his girl; he'd made her feel safe, and cosseted. Now she felt stifled, as if he was trying to treat her as his possession. The feeling gave her the creeps.

Six years was a long time, and she wasn't the same girl he'd left behind. She was all grown up, she owned her own business, she could even walk and chew gum at the same time.

"So, tell me what you've been doing," she said once the waiter had left the table. If he remembered her as she'd been, she remembered him as he'd been, and she saw that memory through her more mature eyes: ask Rick about himself and he could do a solid fifteen minutes without taking a breather.

While they dipped freshly baked bread in flavored olive oil, and while they ate their salads, Rick spoke about his years in Ohio, how he'd climbed the ladder pretty fast but then decided it wasn't the ladder he really wanted to climb. Chessie nodded and said, "Oh" and "Wow" and "Really?" in all the right places, all while silently asking herself: *What did I love about him? What did I see in him that I'm not seeing now? Why didn't I see what a phony he is? Where the* hell *is the main course so I can eat and get out of here? Maybe it isn't too late to call Jace and tell him I got home early and he could come over and we could break our own rules again?*

She came back to attention when Rick reached across the table, took her hand in his, squeezed it. "Chess, I meant what I said on the phone earlier. I don't expect you to forgive me for what Diana and I did to you. It was stupid, cowardly, childish, and I can only say we both paid a heavy price for what we'd done to you. It poisoned our entire marriage."

"I wasn't doing a bunch of backflips myself," Chessie said, and then wished she'd bitten her tongue and kept quiet. She didn't want Rick to think she had been hurt all that badly. "Still, I have to tell you, Rick, I've never been happier. I really enjoy my life the way it is now."

"I know you think you do," he said, and she sat back against the leather booth, pulling her hand away from his. "No, don't do that. I didn't mean it that way. Okay, so I did. You loved me, Chess. I loved you."

Snorting was probably not ladylike, so Chessie just nodded. "And?"

"And I did a terrible thing. I'm not going to blame Diana. It wasn't like she held a gun to my head and said, hey, come with me tonight to Mexico or I shoot. I was young, scared. Marriage is a big step, you know?"

"You took it with Diana," Chessie pointed out, waving away the plate of spaghetti the waiter was about to set in front of her. "We've had a phone call," she told the waiter. "Granny took a turn for the worse and we have to leave. Could you please just box up our dinners for us and get our check ready? Thank you."

The waiter offered his condolences and withdrew.

"Chess? What are you doing?"

Chessie put both hands on the edge of the table, holding on to her composure, and said, "Look, Rick, this isn't working. I accept your apology, but don't ask me to swallow a bunch of—a bunch of horse hooey about why you did what you did. Because, you know, it turns out I really don't care why you did it. You did it. It's over. I've moved on. Period."

"But I haven't, Chess," he said, those gorgeous eyes of his looking lost and wounded. "It didn't work with Diana because all I could think about was you. What I'd done to you, how I'd misled you. How the very last thing you ever said to me was that you loved me and couldn't wait to be my wife. I love you, Chessie, I've never stopped."

Tears stung at the back of Chessie's eyes. She'd spent a year, maybe longer, dreaming that Rick would realize his mistake, recognize Diana for the duplicitous, bloodsucking bitch she was, going after her best friend's fiancé. It had been the worst, most heartbreaking, soul-crushing, empty time in her life.

Any lingering traces of the hurt, the anger, the resentment she hadn't realized she'd still been harboring, drained out of her. This man sitting across from her was a stranger, someone she realized she'd never really known. "I'm sorry, Rick," she said softly. "I'm so, so sorry."

"There's someone else?"

Chessie wasn't about to tell him about Jace. If she said yes, there was someone else, then Rick might think he still had a chance, that all he had to do was convince her that he was the better man. She wanted this to end here. It had been over for a long time, and now it had to end.

"No, Rick. No one. I just stopped loving you. I don't hate you, I'm not angry with you. I forgive you. But I don't love you. I don't feel anything for you except to wish you a happy life. Please, take me home."

He only nodded, perhaps not trusting his voice, and they were silent for a long time, until they were only two blocks away from the salon.

"Chessie?"

Oh, please, just get me home. Don't talk—no more talking. "Yes?"

"Chess, look at me," Rick said as he turned the corner. "Please. Just look at me while I say this. I need to say this before we get back to the—"

Chessie had reluctantly turned to look at him halfway through whatever it was he seemed so intent on saying to her. That's why she saw the large red SUV hurtling toward them, about to hit them broadside. Rick hadn't stopped at the stop sign.

"Rick! Look out!"

But she knew her warning had come too late.

"Oh, my God!"

Chessie got to her feet in the Emergency Room, holding out her hands, hoping to stop Marylou from throwing her arms around her.

"Easy, Marylou. I'm a little sore in spots," she said, backing up, trying to smile.

"A little sore? You're covered in blood! Ted, look at her, she's covered in blood! Why are you sitting out here? Find a doctor, Ted, find six doctors. You donate to this hospital, pull some strings."

"Marylou, honey, I'm fine, and all checked out. Okay, the bruises, they're not so fine. But this isn't blood," she said with a wave of her hand indicating the red stains on her clothing. "It's just spaghetti sauce. I was holding two takeout packages of spaghetti and meatballs in my lap when we were hit."

Marylou tried to squint disbelievingly at her, which didn't work, and then touched a fingertip to one of the larger splotches on Chessie's blouse before putting it to her own mouth. She tried to wrinkle her nose, which worked better than her attempt at squinting, but not by much. "Too much basil," she announced, and then collapsed onto one of the uncomfortable plastic chairs found in Emergency Rooms all across the country. "Oh, Chess, I was so scared."

Ted offered to go to the cafeteria, get them all coffee, and Marylou kissed the hand he'd rested on her shoulder.

"He's my rock. He told me over and over again, all the way here, if you were able to call me then you couldn't be dying. Chess, I don't know what I'd do if anything ever happened to you." She pulled out a linen handkerchief and dabbed at her tear-wet eyes. "You're the sister I never had."

Chessie sat down, put an arm around Marylou's shoulders. "I thought you said you were old enough to be my mother."

Marylou replaced the handkerchief in her purse and snapped it shut. "Must you remember everything I say to you in weak moments? Now, who hit you? And where were you going? You told me you were going straight home to shower and watch television."

"You! What have you done to my Ricky?"

"Oh, boy," Chessie grumbled as Adele Peters stormed through the automatic doors and into the Emergency Room, pointing a finger straight at her. She was just as Chessie remembered her except, as Rick had said, being *more so.* Adele had always intimidated Chessie. But that was then, and this was now. "All we need now are some clowns and a dancing bear."

She got to her feet. "Hi, Adele. You'll want to go back and be with Rick before they take him to surgery."

"Surgery!" Adele clasped her hands to her chest. "This is all your fault."

"Yup, all my fault Rick refuses to wear a seat belt. All

my fault he didn't look left-right-left before heading into the intersection. I take full responsibility, seeing as how I was in the passenger seat and not behind the wheel. Look, Adele, he has a compound fracture of his left arm, a broken right wrist and a concussion, which could have been worse. After bouncing off the window, his head landed pretty much on the takeout containers. He'll be all right. Let me take you to the nurse and she'll buzz you back there to see him."

Adele looked as if she had something else to say, but then simply nodded and followed Chessie, who turned her over to one of the women working behind a desk just outside the closed double doors.

That hadn't been so bad; Adele seemed to respond to a clear voice of command. Now came the hard part. Returning to where Marylou waited for her, her mouth still pretty much open in shock.

"I can explain," Chessie said weakly as she sat down once more.

"And you're going to," Marylou told her, folding her arms across her chest. "Boy, are you going to explain."

Because it had been a long day, and something told her it was also going to be a pretty long night, Chessie first tried redirecting her friend. "Did you know, Marylou, that when you're in an accident going only thirty miles an hour, it's like you just fell headfirst from a three-story building? Oh, and if you're not wearing your seatbelt and it's a front-end collision and the air bags deploy, it's like colliding with something going two hundred miles an hour? Unbelievable, huh? The doctor explained it all to me. Luckily for Rick, it was a side impact and his air bag didn't, you know, deploy. Otherwise, he might be wearing his nose behind his ears right now. Marylou, stop looking at me like that. You're making me nervous."

"Ms. Burton?"

Saved by the bell. Well, the nurse.

"Yes?" Chessie said, getting to her feet, only wincing a little with the movement. She'd been very lucky, that's what the doctor had told her. A couple of mild painkillers, a nice hot shower, and she should be fine.

"Your fiancé wishes to see you before he goes to surgery."

Chessie heard the sharp intake of breath behind her.

"Thank you. I'll be right there." Then she turned to Marylou. "It's not what you're thinking. I couldn't have gone back there with Rick, or learned about his condition so I could call Adele, not as just a friend. Saying I was his fiancée got me in."

"Fine. Devious, but I understand devious. But now his mommy is here to hold his hand, so why are you going back there again?"

Chessie looked toward the doors, where the nurse was waiting for her. It was a good question. Why was she going back there? "He's going into surgery, Marylou. He asked to see me, probably to make sure I'm all right. After all, the accident was his fault. I'll only be a minute, I promise. And then you can yell at me all the way home, okay?"

"Just answer this one question, Chess. How long have you been seeing Rick without telling me?"

"Tonight. Just tonight. And I won't be seeing him again."

"Only tonight? All right, I believe you. You're a lousy liar." Marylou smiled. "Maybe I'll only yell at you half of the way home."

Chapter Nine

Jace got to the job site early on Monday, hoping to surprise Chessie with fancy coffee and fancier donuts he'd picked up along the way. They'd had a nice talk on the phone yesterday, but she had turned down his offer of takeout pizza and a rematch Scrabble game while they watched the Phillies on ESPN. She'd said she was tired, and since she wouldn't get much sleep if he showed up—at least she'd admitted that—he'd finally taken her no for his answer and said good-night.

It had been a long night. Almost as long as Saturday night, knowing she'd been paired up with yet another blind date. He'd asked her a few questions, if she'd had a good time or had to use her secret method of intercepting a move the guy might have put on her, but she wasn't talking, except to say, "It wasn't anything to write home about, if that's what you mean. I think they're finally going to give up on me and leave me alone, thank God."

Then she'd said she was really loving her new shower, that it did wonders for any ache or pain, and he started getting a mental picture that pretty much pushed out the thought that she'd been on a date at all.

He used the key to the side door, having somehow forgotten to ever give it back—yeah, right—and let himself into the salon. He was heading for the stairs up to Chessie's apartment, figuring that having surprised her by entering through the bathroom had been funny once, but he probably shouldn't make a habit of it, when Marylou stepped out of nowhere, surprising him.

"Hi, Jace. You're here early."

He slipped the paper bag containing the coffee and donuts behind his back, which was probably stupid. "You, too. Hi."

Marylou sort of leaned to one side, as if trying to peek around him. "What you got there?"

"Nothing," he said, moving his hand in front once more. "Coffee. Donuts. We're going to have to shut off the electricity for a while today, so I thought I'd bring a peace offering along while I tell her."

"Uh-huh," Marylou said, and the Wicked Witch of the West couldn't have smiled more evilly. "That's very thoughtful of you, Jace. I'm not usually here so early in the morning but we've got a huge gown delivery

scheduled— Do you do that often? Bring Chessie breakfast, I mean? Really, that's very nice of you. So, how was
your weekend?"

"My weekend?" *What the hell was going on here?*
"Fine, thanks. You know. Relaxed, took it easy, had lunch
at my parents' house. Got the usual third degree from my
mom and sisters about my life. Kind of like I'm getting
now."

Marylou laughed. "Is that what you think I'm doing?
Giving you the third degree? I'm sorry. I was just trying to find a way to tell you about Chessie and her little
accident."

Jace shot a quick look up the stairs, his heart having lodged halfway up his throat. "Accident? What accident? Did she fall? I told her not to go poking around
the addition until we got all the tools and electrical cords
out of there. Damn it! When did this happen? Is she all
right?"

"She's fine, just a couple of bruises," Marylou assured
him. "The thing is, Jace, she doesn't want you to know.
And it was in the shower Saturday night, not in the addition. She slipped, that's all, banged her ribs against the
shower door handle or something."

"Damn it. I'll have to check that out. That shouldn't
have happened. The floor of the shower is non-slip, and
she didn't have any problem when—" He caught himself just in time, as he'd been about to admit that he and
Chessie had tried out the shower together.

"When? When what, Jace?"

"Never mind," he said, realizing he'd just used Chessie's favorite expression for whenever she didn't want to say something. She'd probably picked it up in the first place just by having the inquisitive Marylou as a friend. Then another thought hit him. "Why doesn't she want me to know? She mentioned me in particular?"

Marylou looked at a loss for words for a moment, but only for a moment. "Why, actually, she doesn't want anybody to know. Chessie's a very private person, and one of her biggest failings—not that she has many, you understand—is that she hates to admit that sometimes she can be a bit of a klutz. We tease her about it. I mean, she's been known to trip over her own shadow. Anyway, she's not going to tell you about this, but I thought I should so that maybe you can do what you said. You know, look at that shower, see if there's a way to make it safer for our little Ms. Grace. Maybe one of those grab bars like they have for old people? Not that I'd know about those, of course, although I do hear there are designer models now."

"I'll check my catalogs," Jace told her, just wishing she'd go away so he could go upstairs and see how Chessie was doing.

"That's great, I knew I could count on you. Just remember—she really doesn't want you to know, so even if she does feel guilty and feels the need to go into embarrassing detail, make it easy on her and tell her I opened my big mouth and you already know and that everything's fine. Okay?"

Jace looked at Marylou as he tried to sort everything out in his head. "I can know, but I can't know?"

"Exactly! And who said men don't understand these things? Ah, there's Julio's horn, warning me that he's here. Julio's our delivery-service driver. Cutest tush in creation, I'm telling you, and his knees aren't so bad in those shorts he wears, either. Big gown delivery today, Jace, but I think I already told you that. Busy, busy day, but we'll try to get all the boxes out of your way as soon as we can."

"Uh-huh," Jace said, still trying to figure out what the hell was going on. Maybe he should just take Carl's advice, and never ask for explanations because it was simpler, and safer, to go with the flow when women got crazy ideas in their heads. Carl had been married for a long time, so he was probably an expert.

He headed up the stairs two at a time, and knocked on Chessie's door. Waited. Knocked again. "Chess? Chessie, it's me, Jace."

The door opened a second later, and there she was. Her cheeks were a little flushed, and she had a dot of toothpaste at the corner of her mouth, but otherwise, she looked fine. No facial bruises at least.

"Hi," she said rather breathlessly. "I was…I was just— Come on in. What's in the bag?"

He leaned down and kissed her, running the tip of his tongue over her lips. "Yup, I thought so. Wintergreen. Tastes good."

"Nut," she said, grabbing the bag and opening it.

Was she nervous? She seemed nervous. "Donuts? What kind?"

"I wasn't sure," he told her, following her into the kitchen—watching the way she walked, pleased to see she wasn't limping or anything. "So I bought two of each. Two jelly-filled, two crème-filled, two with chocolate icing and sprinkles."

"And each one a favorite of mine in its own way. Be still my heart," she said, grinning at him over her shoulder. "I'm sorry I turned down your very tempting offer last night. Did you watch the game?"

Jace opened the coffee containers while Chessie got out small plates and napkins. "All fourteen innings, yes. You?" Ah, there it was! She flinched a little as she reached for the plates. He guessed he wouldn't be hugging her anytime soon. Poor kid. Poor him!

"I fell asleep right after the Giants tied it up in the eighth. Who won?"

He pulled out her chair for her, which got him a sort of quizzical look before she thanked him and sat down. This was nuts. "We did. Look, Chess, you don't have to hide your winces. I saw Marylou downstairs, and she told me all about it."

She turned so quickly on her chair she cried out, putting a hand to her ribs. "She told you? Why does she always think she knows best? She had no right—"

Wow, Marylou hadn't been kidding. She really hadn't wanted him to know. "Hey, it's okay. I understand. You don't want to talk about it, and that's fine with me. I just don't want you to feel you have to try to hide that you're hurting."

"It's not so bad," she said, still looking at him strangely, as if maybe he'd grown another head. "I mean, the pain pills sort of knock me out, which is why I missed the end of the game, but I haven't even taken one this morning. And you're really all right with that? What Marylou told you."

"Sure, why not?" *Yeah, why not?* "It was an accident. Accidents happen. It wasn't your fault."

"Huh." That's all she said as she sat back in her chair, looking at him. Just "Huh."

Maybe he was overplaying it a little? "It's not that I don't care, Chess," he said quickly. "I do care. I care a lot. But it's nothing that can't be fixed."

She reached across the table and squeezed his hand. "Now I guess I'm glad Marylou told you. I don't know why I was so worried. After all, it was only the one time, and I had a good reason, or at least I thought I did. Anyway, it's over now, just like you said."

Okay, so it was Monday, and he didn't always get his mind running on all cylinders too early on Mondays. But something wasn't computing here. She had a good reason? Who had a good reason to slip in the shower?

"Right. It's over," he said, grabbing one of the crème-filled donuts. "So you really weren't going to tell me? What were you going to do, Chess? Pick a fight with me so I didn't try to hold you and end up hitting on one of your bruises?"

"No. I was just going to suck it up and pretend I wasn't hurting. It seemed safer than telling you about Rick. I'm so glad you understand. If he hadn't pulled out into traffic without looking, you would never have had to know about either him or the accident. I'm just so glad you're all right with it."

Jace had just taken a healthy bite out of his donut, the bite that finally gets you to the crème filling, which was something he loved, but that now felt like a lump of cement in his mouth. He took a sip of the still-too-hot coffee and swallowed, narrowly avoiding getting some of the donut stuck in his throat.

"Excuse me?" he said quietly.

Chessie turned her head to one side, so that she was looking at him out of the corners of her eyes. As if she might decide to bolt at any moment. "You said Marylou told you I went out to dinner with Rick on Saturday night. I wasn't going to say anything at all, but you said Marylou told you. You told me you understood, that it was all right."

"She *told* me you slipped in the shower and didn't want me to know because maybe I'd think that was my fault, and because you're such a klutz. I remember the conversation, Chess. I thought it was pretty strange, even for her. What I don't remember is any mention of this Rick guy's name, or about how you and he were in an accident. Oh, and for the record? No, it's *not* all right."

For a moment, he felt certain that she was going to cry, and he wanted to kick himself for flying off the handle at the mention of Rick's name—not to mention the fact that the bastard had put her life in danger.

"She tricked me into telling you," Chessie said, blinking rapidly, those big blue eyes awash in tears. "I told her. I told her and told her. No, he doesn't have to know. I made her promise not to tell you. She said that was wrong, that you should know and that you'd understand if I explained, but I told her again. No, Marylou. It's over, it's old business. What good would it do? Why even bring it up again?"

"Why? I'll tell you why, Chess." Jace got to his feet, glared down at her, so suddenly angry he was shaking. "Because it would have told me you trusted me. It would have told me you cared enough about what I thought the two of us had going here to trust me with the truth. It would have given me a chance to talk you out of seeing him. Why did you agree to see him, Chess? Curiosity? Or maybe you were doing a little comparison shopping?"

She shot to her feet, sucking in her breath as she quickly clamped a hand to her rib cage. "Comparison shopping? How *dare* you!"

"I don't know, Chess. I guess I'm suddenly daring a lot of things. Like daring to wonder why you had to keep the two of us a secret even after I suggested we stop. Like daring to wonder why Rick also had to be a secret. How many times have you seen him?"

"Once! I saw him once. And I only agreed because he said he wanted to apologize, that's all. He said it would be better if we saw each other for the first time over dinner or something, instead of taking the chance of running into each other in public, where it could be awkward. What he said made some sort of sense, and he was just going to keep calling, so I agreed. I'd let him apologize so he could feel better about what he did, and that would be that, it would be over. Once! I saw him once, and there was no reason to tell you about it. None. And how dare you think I was seeing both of you, keeping you both a secret from each other. That's *sick!*"

"And what the two of us have been doing is healthy?"

She sank back into her chair. "I don't know. In the beginning—we didn't exactly start off like most people who are dating, getting to know each other. I guess I wanted to see where we were going before I told Marylou, told anyone. They're all such matchmakers, and they'd drive me crazy with questions about you and…" She looked up at him, the expression in her eyes bringing him *this* close to forgiving her anything. "And I guess I wanted to keep you to myself for a while longer. You agreed, remember?"

"We were sneaking around like teenagers, having mind-blowing sex—what wasn't to agree with?" *Ah, that was dumb. Beyond dumb. Tell her—tell her how you feel about her. Tell her you'd have nothing left in your life if the accident had been worse, and you'd lost her.* "Keeping secrets from everyone else is one thing, Chess. Lying to me is another. That makes me think this Rick guy is still a part of the picture, and that's why you wanted to keep the two of us your secret. Maybe you still have feelings for the guy. You were going to marry him, remember. So, yeah, comparison shopping. You do see how a man could come to that conclusion, don't you?"

"Yes," she said quietly, so quietly he could barely hear her. "I can see how you could come to that conclusion. But I didn't plan to see Rick again, Jace, I really didn't. And when I finally did see him, I knew immediately that what we'd once had, at least what I thought we'd once had, was over. Truly and completely over. I thought it was, I believed that it was, but now I know for sure."

"But you weren't sure enough to tell me on Saturday that you were going to dinner with him."

She wiped at her eyes with the paper napkin. "What would you have said?"

That stopped him. What would he have said? *Hey, go, have a ball, catch up on old times! Wear that pink blousy thing with the low-cut neck, it's a real turn-on. Give him a big high five from me.* The hell he would have!

"I would have asked you not to go," he said honestly. "Or maybe I would just have followed you, so I could get a look at the guy, make sure he didn't try anything weird on you, give you a hard time. And if he brought you home and you invited him in, I would have probably gone somewhere, gotten myself stinking drunk and picked a fight with anyone who looked even a little like the bastard. I'm a man, Chess. Maybe not the sort of refined, Tennis Anyone men your friends keep trying to push on you, but that's who I am, and that's how a man like me reacts."

"Oh, Jace…."

"Yeah. Oh, Jace. So that's how I feel. The question, Chess, is how you feel. This guy dumps you, and then he comes back to town right before you meet me. Me, who you won't tell anyone about. And then the guy calls you, and instead of saying, sorry about that, I'm involved with another man and, oh, by the way, you're a worthless piece of pond scum, you go to dinner with him, planning to never tell me about the dinner, or about the accident you were in. That's trust, Chess? That's a relationship? Maybe you were right at the beginning. Maybe it was just the sex. I was out-of-the-box different for you, and that turned you on."

"You know that's not true. You have to know that." But she was talking to his back, because he had to get out of the apartment, away from her. He had to go somewhere and think. Maybe he was overreacting. Maybe he was pissed because she hadn't trusted him with the truth. Maybe he was hurting worse than he'd ever hurt in his life because he suddenly knew down to his bones that he loved her, and maybe she didn't love him.

He had to get out of here, think about this.

"I have to check on our other job site," he told her as she followed him down the stairs. "I'll be there for the next couple of days. You need anything, you can talk to Carl."

"Jace, please. Don't do this…."

"Thursday," he said, hating the sad look in her eyes. "I'll be back Thursday afternoon. Maybe by then we'll be able to talk without yelling at each other."

"Chessie, there you are." The teenager, Missy, was walking toward them, holding the cordless phone. "There's this woman on the phone. She says she's calling from the hospital, and she says she's calling because your fiancé can't hold the phone and he wants to know when you'll be coming in to visit."

Jace whirled around to look at Chessie.

"I can explain," she said weakly.

"I'll just bet you can. But you know what, Chess? *Never mind,*" he said, and slammed out the door.

"I have a confession to make," Marylou said as she slipped into the kitchen chair across from Chessie, who was busy drowning her sorrows by dipping chocolate cookies in ice-cold milk. She was almost halfway through the box and her stomach was beginning to feel queasy, but she was doggedly pushing on. Punishment by chocolate. That was a new twist.

"They say it's good for the soul," Chessie said. "Confession, I mean. But I'm here to tell you, Marylou, don't believe everything you hear. Better to tell the truth from the beginning so that there's nothing to confess."

"Maybe. Are you going to eat all of those cookies? A friend would share, you know."

Chessie pushed the box across the table. "Here you go. Go wild. What do you have to confess? I'm the one who lied to everybody. Including myself, come to think of it."

Marylou fished a thin dark chocolate wafer out of the narrow box and broke it in half, then took an infinitesimally small bite out of one half. Marylou could turn one cookie into a half-hour nibble, which was probably why she was a neat size two.

"Mmm, good. I love the recipe on the side of the box. That's the same recipe that's been there for umpteen years, and I've yet to figure it out. You know, how you stack the cookies with that white cream holding them together, and then when you slice it like a log, everything looks so neat and— Okay, okay, don't look at me like that. I'm trying to work my way into this slowly. Just let me start with this, Chess. I had your best interests at heart. Jace's too, come to think of it."

"Hooboy," Chessie said, sitting back against the chair. "That's the kind of statement that rarely ends well. What did you do?"

"I…I, uh, I hatched a plan."

Chessie raised one eyebrow. "Really. And what sort of plan did you hatch this time, Marylou?" she asked in a singsong voice, wondering if she needed to warn Jace. If he'd answer her phone call, that was.

Marylou popped the remainder of the half cookie into her mouth, a clear sign of stress, and spoke around the pieces. "I called it The Bride Plan. I even dragged Elizabeth and Claire into it. And their husbands." She chewed, swallowed, grabbed Chessie's glass and drank the rest of the milk before licking off the milk moustache with the tip of her tongue.

Chessie lowered her head into her hands. "Oh, God, this isn't going to be good…"

But Marylou Smith-Bitters was rarely down, and never really out, so she rallied quickly. "Oh, come on, Chess, it's not like you don't know we've been trying to find someone for you. For *ages*. It's just that this time…well, I had this idea. I didn't even tell Elizabeth and Claire about this one part of the idea, actually."

Chessie lifted her head and looked into Marylou's eyes. "A plan within a plan? How very Machiavellian of you, Mrs. Smith-Bitters. Go on."

"You can look really evil, you know, for someone so sweet butter wouldn't melt in her mouth." Marylou held up her hands in surrender. "All right, all right, I'm going *on*. Each of us was to produce a man for you. I figured that if I got Elizabeth and Claire—yes, and Nick and your cousin—to throw enough men in your path, you wouldn't really notice when I…well, when I slipped another one into the mix. You know, sort of a dark horse I put into the running?"

Chessie banged the side of her fist against the table-top. "I *knew* it! You hired Jace because he's…because he's…"

"Gorgeous? Has a smile that would melt any woman's heart and a body that would melt everything else? Nice, sweet. Intelligent. Different?"

"Different?"

Marylou visibly relaxed, the worst of her confession over, she must have supposed, and continued her explanation.

She came clean about the entire setup with Jace. How she'd worried that her good friend was going to make the bad mistake of going back with her ex-fiancé. How she'd all but lined up a very nice orthodontist for Chessie's next prospective groom but had met Jace Edwards and had had herself a private epiphany.

All of the dates they'd arranged for Chessie over the years had been the same sort of man. All Rick Peters sort of men. Well-groomed, polished, professional sorts. It seemed logical. But maybe none of them had stuck because Rick Peters had been the wrong sort of man for Chessie.

And then along came Jace Edwards.

Serendipity. That's what Marylou had called it.

She hadn't told the rest of The Bride Plan participants about him, just in case she'd been wrong, and Chessie wouldn't be attracted to this more alpha male, this self-made man, this man's man who made his living with his hands.

But, as Marylou told Chessie she'd argued with herself, Chessie was a self-made woman, wasn't she? No stranger to work, ambitious, had built her own business from the ground up. And maybe Chessie wasn't someone who wanted a safe, quiet romance, a safe, quiet husband.

Maybe she wanted a little pizzazz in her life, would welcome a walk on the wilder side, would finally find her perfect match in someone who made her feel alive instead of cosseted. Someone to fight with, to laugh with, to stand beside her instead of in front of or behind her. Someone more elemental, a little rougher around the edges. Someone who, yes, turned her on.

"Pizzazz, Marylou?" Chessie repeated when Marylou had finished her confession by popping the other half of the cookie into her mouth.

"I don't know. Pick a word. It worked, didn't it? Look, I apologize for being sneaky, but I won't apologize for finding Jace Edwards. I also won't apologize for tricking you into telling him the truth about your dinner-and-a-disaster with Rick Peters. You'd have been miserable if you'd kept that hidden from him."

"I know, I know, and you're right. But it has been *days,* Marylou, without a word from him. He says he's coming over here tomorrow. But will he?"

"He loves you, sweetheart," Marylou said confidently. "Men always turn stupid when they first realize they're in love. It's the nature of the beast. Sometimes, you being a case in point, sweetheart, so do women. But he said he'd be back, and I believe him. Especially since he said it to me just this evening, when I made my confession to him. I've had a busy day, cleansing myself of all my sins."

"I don't know if he loves me, Marylou, but I do know he's not stupid. He's right. I should have told you and Elizabeth and Claire about him. I should have told him I was going to meet Rick. Erase that last one. I shouldn't have agreed to meet Rick in the first place."

"Oh, I don't know about that. It's one thing to say something is over, but there's nothing like a little show-and-tell to prove it to yourself. And there wasn't even a momentary tingle?"

Chessie shook her head. "Nothing. He still has beautiful eyes, but a lot of people have beautiful eyes. We could have been two strangers meeting for the first time for all we really knew about each other, other than what we remembered from six years ago. I mean, Rick kept insisting he still loved me, but I think he's figured out that what he was mostly doing was trying to make himself feel better for what he did to me. He also finally figured out that I'm not the same girl he left, that I've got more spine than he remembers, which he doesn't really like all that much."

"While he has less spine than you remember, which you definitely don't like?"

"You're so smart. How do you stand yourself? Yes, he doesn't seem so strong and smart now. More like managing and at times condescending. Maybe because his mother is so domineering, or something. Maybe he wanted to be sure to have a woman he could dominate. I had no idea I'd been that young and stupid. It was an eye-opener, let me tell you."

"My first husband and Rick sound a lot alike. I spent the first two years looking up to him, hanging on his every word, and the last six months wishing he'd just shut up and realize I could speak for myself."

"Yesterday he offered me a check for five thousand

dollars, to help defray the cost of the reception, which had all fallen on me. If that's not trying to buy his way out of guilt, I don't know what is."

"You're kidding. Did you take it?"

"What do you think? I may be an idiot sometimes, but I'm not stupid. That's probably all he ever wanted from me, forgiveness because he's going to be living here now and his conscience was bothering him."

"Good for you!" Marylou clapped her hands. "See? You could be my sister. I would have done the same thing. What are you going to do with the check?"

"I signed it over to Claire for her to use at the community college. You know how she says they never have enough supplies for her child-care classes. You didn't really think I'd keep it for myself, did you?"

Marylou sighed theatrically, then smiled. "I had a momentary lapse in judgment, thinking about that six-year-old car you're driving. But you did the right thing. Did you tell Rick what you did with the money?"

"I did. He's been released from the hospital now, you know. Adele came to take him home, where she'll baby him and spoon-feed him chicken and dumplings and that's that. He knows now that it's over, and I think he's just as relieved as I am. Adele knows it's over, too, which explains why she deigned to kiss me goodbye before wheeling Rick to her car."

"Just think, Chess, you could have married her." Marylou performed a refined shudder.

Chessie laughed. "Not just the man. You marry the

whole family. Yes, we see that more often than we might want to in this business."

"It's good to hear you laugh again. And you've forgiven me for tricking you into telling Jace the truth?"

"It was low and sneaky and yes, I forgive you, because left on my own I wouldn't ever have told him and that wouldn't have been right. I mean, what sort of future would we have had anyway, if I felt I had to hide things from him? I've been doing a lot of thinking these past three days, Marylou, and I was wrong straight down the line."

"Making me right straight down the line. Go on, I like the way this conversation is going."

Chessie smiled, but quickly sobered. "And I was scared. I'm still scared. What if he doesn't believe me? What if he thinks I'm just saying what I think he wants to hear? What if he doesn't come back at all?"

"You don't think he was telling you the truth? Or me, come to think of it."

"I think he wanted to get out of the salon before he was tempted to choke me," Chessie said, and actually laughed, which was probably a sign that she should get some sleep. "I never met anybody so honest about his feelings. So open. Why couldn't I be the same way?"

"You've been hurt, sweetheart, that's why. Once bitten, twice shy, and all of that."

"Jace was bitten. He has just as much reason to doubt his own feelings as I did—do. No, did. I don't doubt them anymore. I really do love him. I thought it might just be the sex. I never experienced anything like that before in my life. I mean, I'd heard about it, but I just figured people were making it all up. And I certainly didn't have any trouble expressing *those* feelings to him. With him. But once I got to know him, then the sex just became a part of it, you know? I mean, a really, really good part, but just a part."

Marylou sighed dramatically. "I want to be twenty years younger all of a sudden. I just don't have that kind of stamina anymore. I never thought I'd be grateful for a man who falls asleep in front of the TV set, but that's what happens, eventually. Which is my way of saying that I'm glad to hear that you see the sex as a part of what you feel for Jace. Real relationships need a stronger base than sexual attraction."

She grabbed her purse. "And now that I sound like an official old lady, I'm out of here. Maybe I can get home before Ted dozes off. Big day tomorrow, Chess. Thursday. Get some beauty sleep."

Because Thursday was a late night at the salon, Second Chance Bridal and Wedding Planners didn't open until noon, but that didn't mean the staff slept in late. Some Thursday mornings were spent inspecting stock for loose lace and sequins, checking to make sure all the shoes were in their correct boxes and catching up on a dozen other jobs that often had to be left to slide during the rest of the week.

But some Thursday mornings were playtime, and this

was one of those Thursdays. Berthe and Millie had un-packed the large Monday shipment and the new wedding gowns were now steamed and pressed and in their plastic hanging bags, ready for their final inspection.

In other words, it was time for the gowns to be tried on, evaluated as to how well they might drape, hang, flatter different body shapes.

Ordinarily, Chessie loved these Thursdays.

Today, however, she kept listening for the sound of hammer and saw, wondering if Jace had shown up. What he'd say to her if he did show up. What she'd say to him.

Or if she'd just burst into tears and behave like a total idiot. She was pretty much betting that's what would happen.

So far, Marylou had tried on three gowns, two that were for more informal, garden weddings—second-time brides often opted for small, outdoor weddings at the local Rose Gardens—and one that actually had a see-through bustier midriff.

"I know I'm not a prude," Marylou said, frowning at the mirror, "but who'd wear something like this?"

"I could put a modesty piece inside," Berthe said, con-sidering the gown overtop her sewing glasses. "It would be easy enough. But some would like it as it is. Not me, however. Too many rolls, not enough midriff."

Everyone laughed, except Chessie, who had just squat-ted down and raised her arms that Millie could drop yet another gown down over her head and then stood up, holding her hands at her waist as Millie secured the concealed zipper.

"I didn't order this," she said, feeling breathless, although the gown fit her perfectly, almost as if it had been made especially for her. "It's…it's, um…" She cleared her throat, which had become suddenly clogged, somehow.

She'd pulled her burnished curls up into a semi-topknot, so that her hair was out of her way, and suddenly the casual style, her brow clear, her eyes accentuated, seemed somehow high fashion.

Couture. Like this gown.

"You like it?" Marylou's voice seemed to come to Chessie from somewhere far away as she stroked her hand across the small, old-fashioned fabric roses that ran across the strapless, semi-heart-shaped upper edge of the bodice. More crushed fabric roses, larger ones, were artfully placed on the full skirt of the ballgown made of a soft, ecru, tone-on-tone alençon lace that lay in three tiers over refined balloon ruffles of *peau-de-soie* that was the same as the *peau-de-soie* that encircled her from beneath the bodice to the dropped waist, making her own waist all but disappear.

"Turn around, Chessie," Millie said. "You have to see the back. It's gorgeous. Just the hint of a train. A sweep train, yes? I think I'm getting the terms down. Oh, but what a beautiful gown! It makes you glow."

And Chessie obeyed, like a automaton given an order. The train was just a sweep, yes, exactly the sort she felt suited her best. And now Berthe was pinning a long, narrow veil just up and under Chessie's topknot. Again, perfect. A simple veil, with no lace, no ornamentation. Nothing to take away from the understated splendor of the gown.

She wanted to tell someone to unzip her. She wanted to wear this gown forever, never take it off, never lose this feeling, a feeling she'd never felt before. The color, the style, the way her fair, slightly freckled skin matched the more whimsical addition of the roses. The way her hair was no longer stupid old red, but a deep, rich copper. The way her eyes had become so much more than simply blue.

She felt beautiful. She was beautiful. A fairy-tale princess come to life.

She wanted to laugh. To twirl. To curtsy to her reflection. To dance the night away in Jace's strong arms.

She began to cry.

"Ah, sweetheart," Marylou said, quickly gathering her into her arms. "It's all right. Everything is going to be all right, you'll see. He loves you. You love him. And this is your gown. I've had it hidden at home forever, waiting for this moment. That's how sure I am, sweetheart. You're going to be the most beautiful bride in the world, and Jace is going to be the proudest groom."

Marylou stepped back, accepting a handful of tissues from Millie (who was also crying), and handed half of them to Chessie. "All right, enough of this. Wait until you see the gown I bought to be your matron of honor. I am going to be matron of honor, aren't I? I mean, I could be best lady and wear a tux—people do that sometimes. But I'd really much rather wear the gown. Come on, Chess, smile! This is your gown, Jace is your man, and we're heading straight for the happily ever after I've always wanted for you."

"Oh, Marylou…" Chessie wiped at her eyes and then took one long last look at the gown. "I've got that cart-before-the-horse feeling again," she said, and sighed. "Let's take this off for now, and try on the rest of the shipment. The real shipment. Later, Marylou, either I'll thank you with all my heart or ask you to just slit my wrists for me."

Marylou took her cue and quickly got back to business, probably mentally fist-pumping and declaring her plan a success. "Thatta girl! Berthe? Put her in the ivory silk with the hat. I've been dying to see that hat on somebody."

Chessie directed one last long look at the gown—her gown—before Millie zipped it into its bag, and then got back to business. This next gown, the last of the morning, was quite lovely, definitely a perfect second-wedding gown, and just right for a garden wedding.

"It's pretty," she told the other women. "The same designer, yes? Although I do have a faint yearning to hunt up one of those shepherd's crooks and tie a big bow to it, sort of like a drawing I once saw in a book of fairy tales. Oh, God, what's that?"

"This," Marylou said triumphantly as she settled the huge round lace-and-tulle-bedecked thing on Chessie's head so that it sat at an angle, "is a picture hat. The mother of all picture hats, actually. You could get married in the morning, go to the Kentucky Derby in the afternoon. Or serve dinner on it," she ended, stifling a grin.

"It will take a much more sophisticated bride than me to carry it off," Chessie said, lifting the too-long skirt and heading out of the dressing room so that she could stand on the pedestal in the reception area, to get a better look at the flower-bedecked train in the larger three-way mirror. "It's gorgeous from the back, isn't it? I feel like a little girl playing dress-up in my mother's clothing. All I need now are ten or twelve necklaces hanging around my neck and a pair of shoes six sizes too big for me on my feet."

"This gown is beautiful, will be beautiful on some other bride. But we know it's not your gown. We've seen your gown."

"Marylou, I wish you hadn't done that, you know," she said as she headed back down the hallway toward the dressing room. "It's the groom who's important on a woman's wedding day. Not the gown. That's one lesson I learned the hard way. Although I will say that the thought of never wearing that gown again is breaking my heart. What time is it?"

"I was hoping you wouldn't ask that. It's nearly noon."

Chessie lifted her chin, bit her bottom lip so that it wouldn't tremble. "And he's not here yet. Maybe because he isn't coming. Maybe because he thought it over and he can't get past the fact that I didn't tell him about Rick, that I was never going to tell him about Rick. I love Jace so much, Marylou. I didn't know what real love was until him. Damn it, how can someone who means next to nothing to me have the power to destroy my happiness? *Twice*."

"That's the stupidest hat I ever saw."

Chessie's eyes went so wide she was surprised they didn't pop out of her head and go bouncing across the floor.

"Timing is everything, as someone extraordinarily brilliant once said. Wow, I think that might have been me," Marylou told Chessie as she walked past her, patted Jace on the cheek, congratulated him on being exactly where she'd wanted him to be exactly when she'd told him to be there and then ushered the other two women into the stockroom.

Chessie turned around so quickly she nearly tripped over the too-long gown. "Wait! Marylou, wait. Come back here, everybody. Get me out of this gown." She glared at Jace, who was standing there looking knee-meltingly gorgeous in a designer tuxedo and grinning like some kind of idiot. Some wonderful kind of idiot.

"You're looking at the tux, right? I don't understand it, either, but Marylou can be very convincing. Either that, or I'd have said yes to anything so she'd shut up. As for getting you out of that gown? I think they think I can handle that. And you can figure out how to get rid of these studs for me. You know, get in some practice before the real thing?"

"You don't want to marry me, Jace. You're mad at me. And I don't blame you."

"Right. I'm mad at you. Glad you reminded me. I was so busy being mad at myself for being an ass, I think I forgot."

"Mad at yourself? But I'm the one who lied to you."

He walked over to her, took her hand. "And I'm the one who lied to himself. Chess, the moment I first saw you, I knew."

She tried desperately not to swallow her tongue. "You knew what?"

"That I was going to love you. That I was going to do everything in my power so that you'd love me. But that's not something that comes easy to guys, Chess, or at least not to me. So I told you I wasn't looking for a committed relationship, trying to make myself believe it. Then you came right back with how you weren't looking for any kind of relationship, and I knew either I had to keep playing along or take the chance of scaring you away forever. So if we're tossing blame around here, let's say I deserve my share."

Chessie closed her eyes just as a single tear escaped to run down her left cheek. "I love you, Jace. We're both probably certifiable, but I do love you."

"I love you, too. Now come on, we can go get each other out of these clothes and apologize to each other some more."

"Come on? Come on where? Jace, put me down! You can't carry me upstairs like this. I have to get out of this gown. I have to open the shop in a couple of— Oh, never mind."

Epilogue

He kissed her hair. He kissed her closed eyelids, the tip of her nose. He lingered for an eternity at her mouth, tasting her, teasing her, drinking her in.

They'd undressed each other slowly in the living room. Well, except for that damn hat. The hat he'd gotten rid of pretty quickly. The gown was now carefully laid out on the couch, the tuxedo not faring quite so well; they'd probably have to go hunting studs later.

But now they were in the bedroom, in their own private Eden, and the rest of the universe did not exist. That was one of the most wonderful things they shared, this ability to concentrate on each other, becoming part of each other, as if they were the only two people in the world.

The lightly freckled skin on her shoulders was velvet,

smooth and soft beneath his hands as he followed the line of her throat with his mouth, traveling her body slowly, inch by inch, telling her without words how much he cherished her, loved her, how she completed his world.

She sighed against him, her body fitting his so perfectly, the tears in her eyes bringing tears to his own.

"I love you," he said. Three simple words. Three simple words that meant so much. "I love you."

"I love you, too. I want to love you forever."

He moved a hand down her body, pressed his palm against her bare belly. "I want my child here. Our child. Our children. And at least one of them a little girl with red hair the color of new copper. Can you arrange that?"

"It might take a little practice, but we could probably make a start on that today," she told him, and then moaned softly as he skimmed his hands over her, cupping her hips as she raised herself to him. "You make me ache for you, to feel you inside me, to know our child soon could be growing inside me. I'm never whole without you. I've lived my entire life not realizing I'd never been truly alive."

"We start living today, Chess. No more yesterdays, only today, and all our tomorrows." He slipped his hand between her thighs, glorying in how ready she was for him, how she seemed to know he would take his time with her today, and that this was all right with her, that she welcomed his slow seduction, wanted to draw out the inevitable until the sweetness mixed with the passion and at last took control.

He caressed her, worshipped her with his hands and mouth. She sighed with him, moved with him, traced his rib cage with her fingertips, igniting small fires along his nerve endings. And all so slowly, because they had all the time in the world, because this was not sex. This was making love from love.

Chessie pressed butterfly kisses against his chest, her breathing becoming more shallow, quicker. Their need for each other growing stronger. She pushed slightly away from him, looking at him questioningly. "Would...would it be wrong of me to say that this is even better than hot monkey sex? Not...I mean, not that we necessarily have to give that up...."

He laughed against her mouth, because laughter was a part of love, and then he raised himself above her and slowly sank into her, their eyes locked together even as their bodies merged and became one.

They'd both been hurt. They'd both worked hard, fought for everything they had. They understood each other. And, together, they'd learned something else.

Without love, nothing else mattered. Without love, there was no success or failure; there was nothing without love. A love to share, a love to grow deeper with each passing day; a life to share, a life that would grow richer every day.

Two months and three days later, Chessie Burton and Jace Edwards became man and wife.

There wasn't a glue-gunned ribbon in sight.

Chessie wore the ecru gown; Marylou wore pale green silk.

Nobody wore the hat.

Seven months and six days after the wedding, a little red-haired cherub took up residence in a bassinet in the workroom that had been converted to a nursery until Jace completed construction on the future residence of Chessie and Jace and Jason Edwards.

As Chessie had told Jace as he looked in love and amazement at his newborn son, "I warned you it might take some practice…."

* * * * *

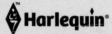
Harlequin®

COMING NEXT MONTH
Available April 26, 2011

SPECIAL EDITION

REQUEST YOUR FREE BOOKS!

2 FREE NOVELS PLUS 2 FREE GIFTS!

❧ Harlequin®

SPECIAL EDITION

Life, Love & Family

YES! Please send me 2 FREE Harlequin Special Edition® novels and my 2 FREE gifts (gifts are worth about $10). After receiving them, if I don't wish to receive any more books, I can return the shipping statement marked "cancel." If I don't cancel, I will receive 6 brand-new novels every month and be billed just $4.24 per book in the U.S. or $4.99 per book in Canada. That's a saving of at least 15% off the cover price! It's quite a bargain! Shipping and handling is just 50¢ per book in the U.S. and 75¢ per book in Canada.* I understand that accepting the 2 free books and gifts places me under no obligation to buy anything. I can always return a shipment and cancel at any time. Even if I never buy another book, the two free books and gifts are mine to keep forever.

235/335 SDN FC7H

Name	(PLEASE PRINT)	

Address		Apt. #

City	State/Prov.	Zip/Postal Code

Signature (if under 18, a parent or guardian must sign)

Mail to the **Reader Service:**
IN U.S.A.: P.O. Box 1867, Buffalo, NY 14240-1867
IN CANADA: P.O. Box 609, Fort Erie, Ontario L2A 5X3

Not valid for current subscribers to Harlequin Special Edition books.

Want to try two free books from another line?
Call 1-800-873-8635 or visit www.ReaderService.com.

* Terms and prices subject to change without notice. Prices do not include applicable taxes. Sales tax applicable in N.Y. Canadian residents will be charged applicable taxes. Offer not valid in Quebec. This offer is limited to one order per household. All orders subject to credit approval. Credit or debit balances in a customer's account(s) may be offset by any other outstanding balance owed by or to the customer. Please allow 4 to 6 weeks for delivery. Offer available while quantities last.

Your Privacy—The Reader Service is committed to protecting your privacy. Our Privacy Policy is available online at www.ReaderService.com or upon request from the Reader Service.

We make a portion of our mailing list available to reputable third parties that offer products we believe may interest you. If you prefer that we not exchange your name with third parties, or if you wish to clarify or modify your communication preferences, please visit us at www.ReaderService.com/consumerschoice or write to us at Reader Service Preference Service, P.O. Box 9062, Buffalo, NY 14269. Include your complete name and address.

*With an evil force hell-bent on destruction,
two enemies must unite to find a truth that turns
all-too-personal when passions collide.*

*Enjoy a sneak peek in Jenna Kernan's next installment
in her original* TRACKER *series, GHOST STALKER,
available in May, only from Harlequin Nocturne.*

"**W**ho are you?" he snarled.

Jessie lifted her chin. "Your better."

His smile was cold. "Such arrogance could only come from a Niyanoka."

She nodded. "Why are you here?"

"I don't know." He glanced about her room. "I asked the birds to take me to a healer."

"And they have done so. Is that *all* you asked?"

"No. To lead them away from my friends." His eyes fluttered and she saw them roll over white.

Jessie straightened, preparing to flee, but he roused himself and mastered the momentary weakness. His eyes snapped open, locking on her.

Her heart hammered as she inched back.

"Lead who away?" she whispered, suddenly afraid of the answer.

"The ghosts. Nagi sent them to attack me so I would bring them to her."

The wolf must be deranged because Nagi did not send ghosts to attack living creatures. He captured the evil ones after their death if they refused to walk the Way of Souls, forcing them to face judgment.

"Her? The healer you seek is also female?"

"Michaela. She's Niyanoka, like you. The last Seer of Souls and Nagi wants her dead."

Jessie fell back to her seat on the carpet as the possibility of this ricocheted in her brain. Could it be true?

"Why should I believe you?" But she knew why. His black aura, the part that said he had been touched by death. Only a ghost could do that. But it made no sense.

Why would Nagi hunt one of her people and why would a Skinwalker want to protect her? She had been trained from birth to hate the Skinwalkers, to consider them a threat.

His intent blue eyes pinned her. Jessie felt her mouth go dry as she considered the impossible. Could the trickster be speaking the truth? Great Mystery, what evil was this?

She stared in astonishment. There was only one way to find her answers. But she had never even met a Skinwalker before and so did not even know if they dreamed.

But if he dreamed, she would have her chance to learn the truth.

*Look for GHOST STALKER by Jenna Kernan,
available May only from Harlequin Nocturne,
wherever books and ebooks are sold.*